MW01136758

All That Escapes
A Post-Apocalyptic EMP Survival Thriller

JACK HUNT

DIRECT RESPONSE PUBLISHING

ISBN: 9781694338495

Also By Jack Hunt

The Renegades
The Renegades 2: Aftermath
The Renegades 3: Fortress
The Renegades 4: Colony
The Renegades 5: United
Mavericks: Hunters Moon
Killing Time
State of Panic
State of Shock
State of Decay
Defiant
Phobia
Anxiety
Strain
Blackout
Darkest Hour
Final Impact
And Many More…

Dedication

For my family.

Prologue

The ambush was set. Camouflaged, a group of heavily armed men crawled toward the tree line either side of U.S. Route 1. Their target was a convoy of three military Humvees.

A cool morning breeze blew in off Penobscot Bay, rustling the leaves around them in Moose Point State Park. Nervousness roiled in the pit of his stomach as Ray Ferguson's finger twitched near the trigger of the M16. He never wanted to kill anyone, especially military, however the odds were high that blood would be shed. The truth was it shouldn't have come to this but when word spread that martial law was in effect across all major cities, he knew it was only a matter of time before Belfast, Maine, fell under government control.

"The target is approaching," Edgar Barrow said.

Ray unclipped the radio and brought it to his lips. "Roger that."

Ray nudged Lee, his brother, an overbearing man in his early forties with a buzz cut and hard mileage in his eyes. Like many in their group, he was ex-military, a man who'd served his country only to be spat out the other side with little to live on. It was a harsh reality that was all too familiar. Lee rose from his position and clicked on and off a small red flashlight, pointing to the other side of the road where five more of the group were waiting for the signal.

All of their camo-striped faces were a picture of concentration.

Before the blackout, the media had pegged them as extremists, no thanks to the Southern Poverty Law Center, which said they were against Muslims and immigrants and had listed them among 273 antigovernment groups in the U.S., however, that wasn't the truth. Maine Militia were law-abiding patriots whose sole purpose was to protect the rights of the American people from all enemies, both foreign and domestic.

And right now the rights of Belfast were being trampled upon. It was a pity. They had worked so hard over the last five years to fight against a skewed public perception by appearing in Memorial Day parades and speaking one on one with residents.

Politics, religion, racism, none of that came into the equation. And yet the term militia still caused a negative reaction in the minds of Americans.

In his mind they were no different than the militia known as the civil defense. It was back then that local militias had prepared Americans in case of military attack. They had been relied upon to protect civilians during the French and Indian and Revolutionary Wars. And because everything functioned at a local level, and citizens participated in annual militia musters — they were accepted, celebrated and revered as the citizens army.

That's why he believed their aim was to back up the National Guard and take care of the American people.

It had been one hurdle after another, an uphill battle that hadn't been helped by the arrests of men in connection with the recent bombing of a Minnesota mosque. The same men who had been part of a skewed Three Percent Militia group in Illinois, the same group who had encouraged people to take up arms against the government.

The SPLC had jumped all over that and as usual threw every militia group under the bus including them. It wasn't long before the term "domestic terrorism" was being used.

Terrorism?

They weren't the threat.

And they certainly weren't racist.

They were here for the people. It had always been about the American people.

As a group they focused on tradition, survival, being prepared and community service, not recruiting civilians and putting them through dangerous training scenarios to take on the government. As he had told the local news, they were all about allegiance to the Constitution, that's all.

And that's why it pained him to have to do this.

Nevertheless it had to be done.

The mission was simple: Take back the supplies the military were taking from the people of Belfast. Ray belly-crawled forward and brought up high-powered binoculars as the caravan of three armored Humvees snaked around the final bend in the road.

His eyes roamed over the telephone poles brought down to block the passage. With the high winds they'd had over the past few days it would have been easy to assume it was the work of Mother Nature. It wasn't.

Over the radio, Ray gave his team instructions to hold.

He was familiar with how the military would respond to this. It was all about timing.

The first vehicle eased off the gas and came to a stop a few feet from the poles. Four National Guardsmen leapt out, two took up offensive positions while the other two went to inspect the obstruction. "Hold," Ray said in a whisper.

It would take more than two to move the poles. A hand went up from one of the military guys, and Ray's eyes bounced to the two vehicles. They shut off their engines and eight more guys hopped out. They were outnumbered by two but it didn't matter, not for what he had in mind. He glanced at his men, their faces, alert, tactical and strained. "Wait for it," he said into the radio.

One by one, the soldiers on the road removed their rifles and propped them up beside the Humvees as they jogged up to the telephone poles to help move them out of the way. As soon as the last one stepped away from his rifle, Ray gave the signal and his group launched the attack.

From both sides of the road they blasted out of the tree line at a crouch.

Short, sharp bursts of diversionary fire from M16's clipped the ground near the feet of the men and caused them to fall back, away from their vehicles, away from their weapons. They had handguns but they would have been fools to go for them. There was no cover. Nothing to fall behind. The attack was so swift and unexpected that hands instantly shot up in surrender.

"On the ground. Now!" Ray shouted.

His team fanned out and bellowed orders for the guardsmen to get on the ground. They emptied a few more rounds while two of his men gathered up their rifles. Ray and Lee moved toward the group.

His men rushed in and relieved them of their handguns.

"Faces down," Lee said. "We are not here to harm you. All we want is what you have taken from the people of Belfast."

A cocky son of a bitch lifted his head. "You are making a big mistake. This jurisdiction is under martial law. We have orders."

"To steal what belongs to another? To trample our constitutional rights? If you want fish, *you* fish. Our people are not doing the hard work for you. You want our guns, try to take them. But don't expect to make it out alive."

"Listen," the cocky guy said in a demanding tone.

Ray dropped down to his level and yelled in his face. "No! You listen. I want you to go back to the FEMA camp and tell them that this ends today. If you try to come back and take what we have, the outcome won't be good. This is your final warning."

"Buddy, you have no idea who you are messing with."

Ray squinted at him. "Neither do you. Now get your men up and move those posts."

"You want us to do it?"

"Did it sound like a question?" Ray replied. Slowly the group of twelve rose to their feet and under the instruction of their platoon leader they moved the telephone poles out of the way. Ray shouted over his shoulder. "Lee, how we doing?"

"All good."

They had moved the fresh fish, guns and medical

supplies from the two vehicles and loaded them into the last, the one they planned on taking and putting to good use. "Get back into your vehicles," Ray ordered.

"Now who's stealing?" the soldier said.

Ray got almost nose to nose with him. He glanced down at his name tape. "Johnson. Call it interest for the goods you took last week, and the week before that. Now go. Get the fuck out of here." Under the watchful eye of his team, the guardsmen hustled to the vehicles and crammed themselves inside like sardines in a tin. The engines roared to life and the National Guard rolled out, leaving them with a Humvee full of goods. A few cheers came from the men. A smile flickered on Ray's face. They'd done it and without killing one soldier.

He turned to Lee. "See, brother, I told you it could be done."

"Yeah, today. But tomorrow might be another story."

"We'll deal with that when we get to it. For now, have Donnelly take the truck back to Belfast and distribute it out," he said heading back toward the tree line.

"Ray."

"Yeah?"

"You know there will be backlash from this."

"I expect there will."

"Next time they'll bring more. Maybe we should stay on the move."

"And go where?"

"Anywhere."

Ray placed a hand on Lee's shoulder. "This is home."

"I'm not talking about going far." He turned and pointed out toward the bay. "The islands. Hell, we could station ourselves in Castine. I doubt they'll head into that sleepy town. We can move back and forth across the bay with ease and keep an eye on Belfast."

"No. We operate from here. They haven't seen our faces," he said from behind the green bandanna covering the lower half of his face.

Ray turned to walk away.

"They've seen mine," Lee said.

Ray stopped and looked back at him. "I told you to

keep it up."

"I did. But they've seen all of ours."

He screwed up his face. "What the hell are you talking about?"

"Everyone in Belfast knows us. We were in the parade. We've spoken with residents. There might be seven militia groups in Maine but we are the only ones in this jurisdiction. They've seen us. And if they've seen us, it's only a matter of time before townsfolk point them in our direction."

"No, you've got it all wrong, brother. People won't throw us under the bus; not once they see what we've done for them."

Lee shook his head. "Not everyone agrees, Ray. Some trust in the government, not us."

Ray walked back to him. "They might not trust us now but they will." He lowered his head. "Look, we'll gather up what we have, and stay low for a while. We'll head across to one of the islands. It will let us stay close enough to remain a fly in the ointment but not so close that we won't see them coming if they decide to react." He tapped his brother's chest. "But I'm not leaving for good, brother. These people need us."

Chapter 1

Max Gray slipped out the window at the break of day, longing to clear his mind. The sun was just beginning to rise, spreading its warm glow across the town of Castine. It was Saturday and yet it didn't seem like it. Since the EMP, nothing seemed the same. His week used to be defined by the weekends. Waking up early, going fishing or heading into town with Ellie. Unlike many of his friends, his relationship with his sister was good. Of course they fought just like any siblings but that didn't last long.

When he wasn't getting out of the house and creating his own adventures, he usually had his head stuck in a video game but even that was a thing of the past. Five and a half months, that had to be a world record. Now it was all about hunting and gathering. He was beginning to understand what cavemen must have felt like foraging for food.

It was exhausting, physically and mentally.

Then there was the sugar crash, he'd experienced it sometime in the first month. Okay, it wasn't as bad as he thought, but still, he was only seventeen, he was used to consuming a large pack of Doritos, sucking down Mountain Dew and eating his way through four candy bars and that was all before lunch.

Now it was dried fruit, fish, vegetables, jerky and nuts.

Not exactly teen food.

He slid down the roof and dropped to the ground. A heavy dew had settled on the grass. He paused there for a moment and listened, hoping his mother hadn't heard. Lately he felt suffocated. It was like she was micromanaging everything he did. *Where are you going? When will you be back? Have Jake go with you.* It was tiresome. Sure, he understood. She was worried something terrible would happen but he would be eighteen in a month and in some areas of the world, that meant he was an adult.

He didn't hear any movement so he adjusted his

backpack on his shoulder, pulled his beanie down and jogged away from the Manor towards a shed where his bike was stashed. He dragged the red mountain bike out, hopped on and pedaled off into the mist that hung low.

Days seemed to blur into one, just an endless stream of trying to keep their heads above water. Survival had become the default state, and with every passing day it had got harder. He missed his father, but most of all he missed Ellie. At least if she was here he wouldn't feel so damn alone. It wasn't that he didn't have friends. There were a few that lived in Castine but he hadn't seen them since the lights went out. Most of the teens his age either bused out to Bucksport High School or George Stevens Academy in Blue Hill, both were about a thirty-minute ride away.

He just wanted one day, one day he could be himself. One day to forget that the world had turned into one big shit burger.

Over the past few weeks Jake been scoping out some of the islands nearby. He figured that they needed to keep their options open. Even with Deputy Daniels and residents policing the town, theft and murders were still on the rise. The Manor was comfortable, but for how long?

Almost everything they needed to live could be gained from the land, the bay and the sky: vegetables, small animals, fish and rainwater.

The trouble was moving away from the manor was just talk, that's because they didn't have just them to think about — there was Rita Thomas, and Tess, and now Sam and Carl who had taken a liking to coming over in the evenings, drinking wine and shooting the breeze with Jake who was now deputized. Talk, talk, talk. That's all they ever did. That wasn't going to get them anywhere, so he figured he'd scout out the islands for them.

Today he had his eyes set on Nautilus Island, but not for the reasons Jake and his mother had talked about it. The place had always intrigued him. It was privately owned by some bigwig with a crapload of money, and there were a number of rumors floating around that the owner fancied himself as a bit of a Hugh Hefner, holding large parties with lots of women, drugs and sex. Others said he was the CEO of some big corporation in Bangor, and the century-old building with tennis courts and king-size pool was only used as a summer retreat. Then of course there was a rumor that some eighteen-year-old self-made millionaire entrepreneur owned it. Whatever the truth was, it was intriguing and he planned on finding out.

Max stood upright on his pedals, gliding down Battle Avenue toward Dyce Head Lighthouse. It was a favorite spot with tourists. They couldn't go in the lighthouse but they could view it from a distance. The tiny white home beside it was private property but there was a sign indicating a path that fed around the back of the barn through the woodland and to steep wooden steps that led down to the waterfront. With so many people leaving Castine after the blackout, he'd taken a small fishing boat from an abandoned home and stashed it among the trees near Dyce Head.

As he swerved, glided and pedaled along the short path, he noticed how hardly anyone was out. He'd only seen two other people that morning. A jogger, and someone walking their dog. That was the strange thing about life after the EMP. People tried to maintain some semblance of a normal life by following a routine. For some that was jogging, working out, for others it was walking their dog or even going to work if their job allowed it. Though the only businesses still operating were fishing companies looking to trade fish in exchange for life's creature comforts. For some that meant candy and moonshine, for others gasoline, whatever was left. Five and a half months into this and there really wasn't much of anything left. Those who did have, squirreled it away and were smart enough not to tell others. Those who did often became the focus of theft.

A warm breeze blew in off the water as Max dragged the ten-foot boat out of the brush, over the rocks and into the choppy waves. He shrugged off his backpack and threw it in before stepping into the boat and firing up the motor. Fortunately, it still had a small amount of gas from whoever previously owned it. He tugged on the pull cord multiple times before it spluttered to life, and water kicked up behind the boat. He eased away from the shore and started to cross the half-mile gap between Castine and Nautilus.

He saw a few fishermen heading out of Castine harbor and others in Penobscot Bay catching fish. Sunlight glistened on the water's surface almost blinding him. Fishermen glanced his way and he raised a hand. An old-timer returned the gesture, having no idea that he was heading for private property. While Max hated trying to survive each day, in a strange way he kind of liked the fact that he didn't have to go to high school. If he didn't have chores to do, and if he had more friends, maybe he would actually like this new world.

Saltwater sprayed in his face. He squinted and looked at the island coming into view. Nautilus Island was shaped like a boot with the top end barely connecting with another island at low tide. The only way to reach it was by boat. He directed the boat towards the 300-foot wooden dock that jutted out from the north side. He was glad to see there were no other boats moored. It meant the island was empty.

As much as he liked living at the Manor, the idea of moving to the 38-acre private island with ocean views seemed more than adventurous, it felt safe and he hadn't felt that way in a long time. Through the trees he could just make out the huge house high up on the bluff, surrounded by century-old sugar maples and tall pines. Nearby was a cluster of buildings.

Excitement rose in his chest as he cut the engine and glided through the water towards the dock. The bow knocked against the wood and he reached up for some rope to moor it. After tying it off, he climbed onto the dock, slung his bag over his shoulder and stood there looking at the island. He couldn't believe he was here. In all the years he'd lived in Castine, he'd only ever seen it from a distance. He couldn't begin to imagine what it must have been like to own it. He stumbled down the rickety dock, curious but at the same time cautious. There was no telling who might be there. With so many home invasions, he knew he was taking a risk venturing onto the island. That's why he kept his gun in the holster. He didn't want to give the owner any reason to shoot him, if they were there.

Max hurried onto the island. The gravel path cut through a lush forest with a tennis court off to the right, and a small Cape Cod cottage on the left. He could see the main house in the distance but was curious about the cottage. Max approached it and peered through the window. No movement. No sounds. No one was home. He twisted the knob. The front door was locked. He went around to see if there were any windows open. None. He figured after five and a half months the place would have been ransacked by now but it was still in tiptop shape. Why hadn't anyone headed over to the island? He considered smashing a window and going inside but his excitement over visiting the main house got the better of him. Jumping down off the front porch he broke into a sprint heading for the mammoth house further inland. He could just make out the creamy gray exterior and brown shingles through the woodland. Sun beamed down through the trees onto his forehead as the end of the path opened up to a large driveway. A golf cart covered in dry leaves from the winter was off to one side. Seemingly, no one had been there since the previous summer. That was a good sign.

Max jogged up to the main door and gave the handle a shake. Locked. He roamed the perimeter of the house, tugging on the windows but knowing that he would likely need to smash one. As he reached the rear of the home he was greeted by the incredible sight of a solar-heated infinity pool covered with a blue tarp that had been rolled out to prevent leaves drifting into the water. "Oh, now this is what I'm talking about." Now he wished he'd brought a towel. Max glanced to the west, towards the pool house. Maybe he didn't need to. He approached the tiny clapboard structure flanked by planters. Beyond the glass double French doors were shelves of towels, and pool equipment. Max took out his handgun, looked around, then used the butt to break one of the glass panels. It shattered sending shards of glass inside. He holstered the weapon and reached in to unlock it. *Klunk.* What a sweet sound. He entered and pulled a thick white towel off the shelf and brought it to his nose, sniffing. Perfect.

Before taking a morning dip he did one more round of the house, just to be on the safe side. Satisfied that no one was home, Max stripped out of his clothes, tossed them on a pool chair and rolled back the tarp to reveal the pristine water. Fully naked, he crouched and dipped his hand below the surface and ran it back and forth. It was surprisingly warm. Max made his way to the diving board, climbed onto it and curled his toes at the end. He bounced a few times, feeling sheer joy. "Woohooo!" he bellowed before doing a dive bomb into the pool. He plunged into the tepid water and emerged wiping his hand over his eyes as he rolled over onto his back and looked up at a bright morning sky. Ah, now this was what it was all about. Forget worrying. Forget spending all the time in survival mode. The world had gone to shit. Why not enjoy the perks that came with it? He did the backstroke to the far end and rested his forearms on the wall. Now if he just had a few bottles of beer, some weed and a female companion it would be heaven.

He pulled himself out of the pool and faced his back to the water. He put his arms up in the air, then down at his side before doing a terrible backflip. The chlorinated water went down his throat and he came up choking.

Once the water was out of his eyes, he looked towards the pool chair, planning to get out and dry off, that's when he noticed his clothes were gone. "What the heck?" He whipped around, turning a full 360 degrees. He'd put them on that chair. Where were they? His heart started pounding. Cold fear shot through him.

"Looking for these?" a male voice asked.

Max twisted to see a kid no older than him perched on the wall beside the hot tub. In one hand were Max's clothes and backpack, and in the other a handgun. *His handgun!* The guy was wearing a dark baseball cap, black sunglasses, a solid olive-green military jacket with gold buttons and a worn ranking patch on the arm. Beneath that was a black T-shirt, and faded jeans tucked into military-style black boots. He held out the gun and turned his hand as if admiring it.

"Yours?" he asked.

Of course it was, he wouldn't leave the house without packing some heat. He'd had a Walther P99 in the holster on his hip and two extra magazines in his backpack to cover his ass if he got into a bind. Even though his mother had been against the idea of him carrying, the recent string of murders and the attack on their home had made her rethink. Besides the obvious reason — personal safety — Jake had convinced her that while it might not have been common in Maine for kids his age to carry a gun, it wasn't uncommon throughout America. In fact it was easier for an eighteen-year-old to get their hands on an AR-15 than it was a handgun. And in rural areas with a strong tradition of hunting, like Minnesota, a rifle could be bought at the age of 14 without parental consent.

Anyway, she agreed on one condition: that he only use it around Jake, at least until he was eighteen. Of course he wasn't going to listen to her. Who in their right mind would leave home without a gun in this shit storm?

Now he wished the damn thing had been waterproof, he could have taken it into the pool with him. He groaned and gave a nod.

The guy's lip curled up. "A Walther P99." He screwed his nose up. "I'm more of a Glock man myself." He grinned at Max before lowering it.

"You live here?" Max asked.

The guy looked around casually with a smile on his face. "Maybe. Maybe not."

"Well, you mind tossing my gear over here?"

He laughed, tapping the gun against his leg. "All in good time, grasshopper. First, a few questions— being as you are trespassing."

"As are you if you don't live here."

"Never said I didn't."

"Ha! But you never said you did," Max shot back, jabbing his finger at him.

The guy stared then got up and began to walk away with his gear.

"Okay. All right. Ask the damn questions." Max sighed, shaking his head.

He returned and sat on a step. "Where you from?"

"Castine."

"What brings you here?"

"Probably the same reason you're here," he replied in a sarcastic manner.

"Answer the question."

"Exploring. You?"

"I ask the questions, you answer them. Got it?"

Max eye rolled. The guy set the gun beside him and reached into his pocket. He retrieved a small tin. Inside was some weed, and rolling papers. He took it out and began to roll himself one while he looked at Max. "You always go swimming butt naked?"

"Always," Max replied. If he was going to ask dumb

ALL THAT ESCAPES: A Post-Apocalyptic EMP Survival Thriller

questions, he'd give him dumb answers. The guy laughed as he licked the paper and rolled one. He twisted the end and placed the reefer in his mouth. He brought a lighter up to it and paused before lighting it. "You went to Bucksport High School. Right?" A flame burst to life and he scorched the end, taking a few hard pulls before coughing hard.

"Yeah."

"I know. I used to sit behind you in math until my parents decided to move to Blue Hill." He blew out a cloud of gray smoke and leaned back, using his one arm for support. He acted so nonchalant. Meanwhile Max was beginning to get cold. He started to shiver; his teeth chattered. "Worst move of my life. But at least the girls are hotter at George Stevens."

What was this kid trying to prove?

"That's debatable," Max replied.

"Oh it's a proven fact. Bucksport is full of hags."

"Yeah, name one?" Max asked finding him amusing.

"Maria West."

Max narrowed his eyes. "All right, I'll give you that."

He burst into laughter and Max couldn't hold his in.

"You done with your twenty questions?"

The kid got up and strolled over with his things and dropped them beside the pool. He extended a hand and Max clasped it. After pulling him out he removed his sunglasses. "The name's…"

"Eddie Raymond. Yeah, I remember you." Max reached for his clothes and put them in front of him. "You mind?"

"Nothing I haven't seen before. Well, nothing that small but…"

Max gave him the bird and walked back into the pool house to get changed. All the while Eddie waited outside, still holding his gun. "You know, I thought I was the only one that came here."

"After today you still might be," Max yelled from inside. Eddie leaned against the door peering in like a peeping Tom. It was really off-putting.

"I've stayed here a few nights."

"Stayed?" Max asked.

"Yeah. Oh that's right, you checked the windows. You won't get in that way. I'll show you." Max reemerged, running the towel over his black hair before tossing it. "Come on, I'll give you a tour."

"Think I can get my gun back?"

"Sure." He removed the magazine and handed it over before leading the way. Max fished into his backpack for a second magazine but they were gone. "Oh, I took the liberty of lightening your load. You'll get them back when we part ways. But I can't have you shooting me in the back, now can I?" he said casting a glance over his shoulder and grinning. They were halfway to the house when they heard voices, multiple, deep and booming. Both of them froze.

Chapter 2

The copperhead struck without mercy, its venom coursed through his hand like molten lava. Landon whipped back, gripping it in agony. At first it had felt like nothing more than a wasp sting until he saw the fang marks and blood on the side of his hand. That soon changed. Pain, frustration, disbelief. All of it culminating at once, overwhelming his mind. Five hundred and forty-three miles of pushing through some of the worst terrain and weather. One and a half months on the Appalachian Trail, making it through countless near-death encounters with small-town thugs, crazy hikers, and unstoppable bouts of hunger — they'd survived it all — then this had to happen. Over halfway. They were making progress. Landon stared in disbelief at the pack he'd laid outside the outhouse of the heavily forested High Point Shelter. Landon stumbled back, air catching in his throat just as the copperhead snake slithered out of his bag and disappeared into the underbrush. It wasn't in there two minutes ago. He was sure of it. He'd put his hand into the bag and retrieved the wipe tablets. How could this be? He staggered as he tried to get to his feet.

"Beth!"

He didn't need to call her, she was already sprinting towards him, bow in hand, ready for the worst. Grizzly was right beside her, panting up a storm. "What, what, what?" she said as her eyes scanned the forest looking for threats. He lifted his hand and her jaw dropped. "No."

"Copperhead. It was in my bag."

He rocked back and forth, the pain was overwhelming.

"Are you sure that's what it was?"

"Yeah." He knew how important it was to know what had bitten him to get the right anti-venom.

"Where is it?"

"It's gone. Over there," he said pointing with his good hand. Grizzly dashed over as if understanding and began sniffing the brush.

She dropped her bow and removed his watch, followed

by the tight raincoat he had on. "We need to get you medical attention and fast." He went to get up and she told him to stay sitting down and to keep his hand above his heart to decrease circulation. "Don't be moving around. You try to move and your heart rate will increase and then the symptoms can get worse."

"Right… but shouldn't I get away from this spot?"

"Billy!" Beth yelled.

Billy, aka Maestro, had turned out to be one hell of an oddball. After saving his ass back in Virginia, they'd barely managed to get a word out of him but get a little alcohol in him, or some weed, and he was like another person. In all honesty, Landon was hoping they would have parted ways by now because his mood swings were starting to worry him. The only thing that seemed to keep him on an even keel was cigarettes. Within a matter of days he'd blown through the pack Landon had given him, and had it not been for a stop in a small town in Virginia, he was certain they might have seen another side to him. Billy wandered over, no urgency in his pace. "Problem?"

"Give me a hand bringing him over to the shelter."

"Can't he walk?"

"What's it look like?" Landon said, losing his rag as blood trickled out of his hand. Within a matter of minutes his hand had started to swell. The pain was excruciating and getting worse by the second. He ground his teeth and rocked his head back groaning in pain. Billy put an arm around his waist and with the assistance of Beth helped him back to the tent. Although his legs were working perfectly fine, his vision was beginning to blur. All the while Beth was talking to him trying to keep him calm.

"Every snake is different. Copperheads aren't the worst and bites can vary in toxicity," she said.

"Am I going to die?"

"No. I mean, you could but few die from these within the first four hours. If it happens it's many hours or even days later. We just need to get some antivenom." She cursed. There had been some in their backpacks before they were taken and in all the towns they'd visited so far their minds were too focused on getting other supplies to think of that.

"He could die," Billy said. "Seen it happen."

Landon started hyperventilating.

"Hey, hey. Calm down!" Beth said. Grizzly sidled up to Landon and curled around him as if trying to keep him calm.

"Really?" Landon asked.

"Oh yeah, death or severe tissue damage can happen. Hell, you could lose a limb. But I doubt that will happen to you."

"Billy. Would you shut up!" Beth said. "You're not helping."

"Excuse me," he replied in a sarcastic tone.

Landon dropped his head forward as they brought him into the shelter. "I'm feeling nauseous. My arm is going numb. I can't breathe." Sweat trickled down the side of his face.

"You're getting worked up. Stay calm. I need to think. Give me a minute to think." Beth paced.

"Didn't your father teach you about this stuff?" Billy asked.

She ignored him as she tried to recall what her father had said about the different types of venom.

"Aren't you supposed to make a cut and suck out the venom?" Landon asked.

"No. That's Hollywood bullshit," Beth said. "Besides, if you have a sore in your mouth, you'll end up with the venom in your system," Beth said. She dug into their new bags they'd picked up since Virginia. They only carried the basics. Beth used some of her water to wash the wound and wrapped a bandage around the bite just as someone might with a sprain. She then left the shelter and returned with a sturdy stick to use as a splint. She stuck it up through the bandage and used a second bandage to prevent his arm from moving.

"What are you doing?" Billy asked.

"It's called pressure immobilization. We need an antidote but in the meantime we can slow the process considerably using this method. This prevents you from using the muscles, and in turn reduces the flow of blood which would send it further into your system. How's that feel? Not too tight?"

"It's fine… but shouldn't we apply a tourniquet?"

"No. That can just lead to more problems. Look, there is a good chance it's just a dry bite and no venom went into your system. But either way, we need to get some antivenom and fast." She fished into her bag and pulled out a map and compass. "I'm going to the nearest town. I'll be back soon."

"Just take me," Landon said.

"No. It will only get your heart rate going and—"

"Why don't I go? You stay with him," Billy said.

Had he said that after they first met him, Landon might have been inclined to let him but his recent behavior had given him cause for concern. He wondered if he'd even come back. "No, you should go, Beth," Landon said. She'd already proven herself in the Blue Ridge Mountains as trustworthy.

Beth focused on the map, laying it out in front of her.

"Shit. The nearest town, Port Jervis, has to be at least two, maybe three hours away by foot. Unless I can find a vehicle, that's not happening."

"And I imagine the hospital isn't operating," Landon said, beginning to think that his luck was running out. They'd had a good run. The fact they'd made it halfway and were still alive was a feat in itself. He looked at the map. "What about here?" He pointed to a farm and a training center nearby. "If you cut through here, that's less than two miles away. Maybe someone has a working vehicle."

"That's south of here. I'd be taking a risk."

He shrugged. "We don't have many options." Landon looked over at Billy. "Billy, you think you can go and check the area where I was bitten? I want to make sure that was a copperhead."

"You said it was," Beth replied.

"Can't be sure."

Billy nodded and headed out. Landon waited until he was out of earshot before he grabbed Beth by the wrist. "I don't trust him."

"Why?"

"I have my reasons. Besides, how did the snake get in my bag?"

"They crawl into a lot of places, Landon."

"The bag was upright. You ever seen a snake go up into a bag?"

She stared back at him. "You want me to stay?"

"No, because I don't know if he would come back and if he did, could we trust he went into town? I mean if he returns without antivenom."

"So I'll take him with me."

"I don't trust him with you. I'd rather he stayed with me."

"Landon. If he wanted to harm us, he's had over a month and a half to do it. It's highly unlikely he'll do it now." Landon dropped his chin. He had so many questions related to the last town they were in and the run-in they had with that hiker. Call it a gut instinct but something was very off about Billy, he just couldn't put his finger on it. "You good?" she asked. "I hate to do this but if I don't get it…"

"I know," he said cutting her off. "Go. Be quick."

Billy came around the corner and stared at Landon as if he'd been standing there the whole time. "Couldn't find it," he said with a deadpan expression.

"Must have got away," Landon replied. "I'm pretty sure it was a copperhead." He averted his eyes from him and Beth looked over to Billy.

"Watch over him. Okay? Don't let anything happen."

"You got it." Billy smiled and Landon felt his stomach sink.

Beth squeezed his good hand, then removed his handgun and gave it to him in front of Billy. He knew what she was doing by the look in her eyes. "You never know. Maybe a bear might come along. Can't be too safe," she before giving a strained smile. She glanced at Billy and then scooped up her bag, got her bow from where she had dropped it, and then took off with Grizzly beside her.

* * *

Beth hurried through the woods using the compass as a guide. She didn't want to leave him but it was that or risk the venom spreading faster through his system if she took him with her. Had the hospital been only a few miles away she might have reconsidered.

"Come on, boy," she said. Grizzly bounded over roots and fallen trees, keeping up with her pace.

As her boots pounded the underbrush and she slalomed around trees, her thoughts went to Landon and his paranoia with Billy. She hadn't seen Billy acting out of sorts. Sure, he was a little strange, and quiet at times, but who wasn't. They'd been through a lot. All of them had. There had been several times he'd had their backs in a few tight spots in Virginia. He could have slit their throats in the night but he hadn't. She pushed the negative thoughts from her mind, it wasn't helping.

It didn't take long to run the two miles through the woods. When she burst out of the dense woodland she was on Greenville Road. They jogged north until she saw a sign for Breezy Brook Farm. Although she was eager to cry out for help, previous encounters with homeowners had taught her to be wary. It wasn't your typical farm. Had there not been a sign she might have considered it your run-of-the-mill home pushed back from the road. There was nothing grandiose about it. A simple two-story home with brown shingles, half vinyl siding and half brick foundation.

Beth hadn't made it a few feet down the driveway when a gun erupted tearing up grass near her feet. Her gaze moved to the top window of the house where she noticed a woman holding a rifle. "That's far enough!"

She jutted over her shoulder with a thumb. "I have a friend who's been bitten by a copperhead. I need to get him medicine from the nearest hospital. Do you have a working vehicle?"

"If I did, do you think I would tell you?" the woman replied. "And besides, you'll be lucky to find a doctor."

Beth squinted. She looked to be in her late fifties, slightly on the robust side with a full head of dark curly hair. "Please."

"Get out of here. Now!"

"I just—" Before she could get out another word, two more rounds tore into the dirt near her feet. She backed up, hands in the air. Grizzly growled and then barked. "All right. All right. We're leaving." She wanted to curse at the woman but how could she? She would have probably done exactly the same thing. Everyone was skittish around strangers.

Not more than two hundred yards down the road was High Point Training Center. Due to the numerous stables and the layout of the grounds, she assumed they trained horses. Getting a little closer to a black-and-white sign, she saw a picture of a horse's head, and text below it advertising training and boarding. She approached the two-story, gray vinyl-sided home expecting to find herself staring down the barrel of a gun but no one attacked her. One short knock. No one answered the door. "Hello!?" She peered in through the window but couldn't see much because of the thick drapes. Pulling her sidearm, she went around the back of the house to make sure someone wasn't out back. Nothing. No one. Grizzly followed her through a gate and over to the stables. She stuck her head inside but there were no horses, no people, not even hay. She pursed her lips and looked at the time on her wristwatch. She considered continuing up the road and checking in on another home but instead she made her way to the back of the house and checked the doors and windows. A window that led into the dining room shifted up. She told Grizzly to wait while she climbed through.

Inside it was musty as though the windows hadn't been opened in a long time. The floors were hardwood, and she could hear a clock ticking.

"Hello?" she muttered just in case someone was asleep. Keeping her handgun close to her she pressed into the house and cleared each of the rooms. No one was home but it looked as if someone had been there recently as a camping stove was still warm, and there were two cups on the counter. Beth headed for a door that led into the garage. She opened it and noticed an old black pickup truck. There were no keys inside. Quickly she returned to the kitchen and scanned the countertops, the table, and a small rack for any keys that looked like they might be for a vehicle.

She scooped up a set that had nine keys on it and made a beeline for the back door to let Grizzly in. Grizzly wagged his tail and began sniffing the floor. "Come on," she said leading him into the garage. She hopped into the truck and was thumbing through the set of keys when she heard tires roll over gravel.

Beth got out and went over to the dusty pane of glass in the garage door. She ran a hand over the glass and saw two guys getting out of a truck, both carrying rifles and heading for the front door.

Chapter 3

Having appliances operate was a luxury they hadn't experienced in almost a month due to a lack of gasoline. A rare commodity, the valuable liquid could only be found inside stranded vehicles, and most in the surrounding area had already been siphoned by locals. The previous day, Jake had been out searching the back roads, and highways beyond Castine, and had returned late in the evening with just enough to keep his Scout ticking over, however he'd insisted she use it in the generator to lift the morale, especially Tess. No one more than Tess could fathom what her husband, Ian, had committed. She'd been with him for years and never once been victim of brutality, that's why it didn't make sense how a seemingly ordinary man could commit such heinous acts.

Though as they reflected on the incident, slowly the pieces fell into place: Ian's long work hours, the huge amount of food and supplies he'd stocked at the house, and a string of women who'd gone missing in the county only a year or two before the blackout. He was living a double life and Tess had been oblivious to it all.

Sara hoisted the five-gallon red canister out the back of Jake's Scout and lugged it over to the shed. "Are you sure about this?" Sara asked as Jake emerged from the house with a cup of coffee. "I'm sure Sam could use it in his vehicle."

"I'm sure they could but for how long? A day or two? No, we have the horses and bicycles now, and enough people helping in Castine to not have to rush from one end of the town to the other." He jabbed his finger. "So don't be telling them. If anyone asks, this is the leftovers from a canister you had forgotten about, okay? Besides, after all you've done helping people, and taking in those from the town, I want to give back."

She smiled, thanked him again and emptied the contents into the generator and fired it up. Oh, it was such a sweet sound hearing it churn away. It was the small things that mattered now.

Janice Sterling and Arlo were the recent additions to the Manor. It had taken a lot of convincing to get Arlo to leave behind the farm but common sense prevailed in the end. They were stronger together. And having Janice there provided Rita Thomas with some much needed company since losing her husband.

"There we go," Sara said stepping back from the generator as Jake sidled up beside her and handed her a coffee. "Thanks." They wandered back to the house and up onto the porch. Sara took a seat on the porch rocker and nursed her coffee, savoring the aroma and letting it bring her senses to life. "So what are your plans for today?" she asked.

"Teresa's having a meeting this morning. She wants to introduce us to some bigwig from FEMA."

"Oh that."

He nodded, shaking his head. "She says that it's just a routine check. They want to know the state of the situation, what infrastructure we still have in place and where the needs are. Seems FEMA is going town to town."

"Seems obvious to me," she said taking a sip of her coffee. "We're in dire straits."

Just as Jake was about to respond, the storm door creaked open and Rita poked her head out. "Max not with you?"

Sara frowned and rose from her seat. "No. Why?"

"I called up to him but didn't get an answer. I went up and his bedroom is empty. I figured he was with you."

Sara put her cup down and made a beeline for the door.

"C'mon, Sara, don't worry. He's probably just gone for a bike ride," Jake said trying to reassure her. It didn't help. She raced up the stairs to his room and flung the door open. His bed had been slept in. Her gaze darted to the window where the drapes were gently blowing. "Max!" She nearly ran Jake over on the way out. "He's gone. We need to find him." Jake caught a hold of her arm.

"Sara. Slow it down. He's almost eighteen. You can't keep him cooped up in here the whole time."

"Is that what he told you?"

He shifted from one foot to the next. "He might have mentioned feeling smothered."

She pursed her lips and hurried downstairs. "I have good reason. You know how many people have been attacked in this town, Jake?" She dashed out of the house with him in her shadow.

"Sara, wait up! There's no point you going out there. I'll go. Let me talk with him. He'll just think you're being overbearing."

She came to an abrupt halt and spun around. "Overbearing? Overbearing!" she bellowed causing a big enough commotion to attract the attention of the other guests in the house. "He's all I have left. Had this event not happened, maybe I wouldn't bat an eye but we are living in a different world now. A lawless one, and we've already overlooked one person and look at what he turned out to be!" Right then her gaze went to the door where

Tess was standing. She lowered her head and walked back in. "Tess. Tess. I didn't mean it like that." She groaned and brought a hand up to her head.

Jake approached her again as she contemplated whether to go searching or wait for his return. Jake continued, "All I'm saying is that…"

Sara threw a hand up. "Jake, I appreciate your help, and your attempts to bond with Max, but you're not his father. I'm all he has and he's already gone through enough as it is. I think I know what's best."

"I know that and I'm not trying to replace Landon."

"Sure seems like it," she said.

Jake took a few steps back and squinted at her. "You know, maybe this was a bad idea. Me staying here."

"Jake. I'm…"

He threw a hand up. "I gotta go. Sam's waiting." He headed for the stable where the horses were. Arlo had brought them from his farm. Jake cast a glance over his shoulder before unlocking the stable and entering. Sara closed her eyes and cursed inwardly. Great. That was two people she'd pissed off and it wasn't even eight in the morning. She turned to see Rita walk back into the house.

While she understood what Jake was trying to explain, it didn't take away the fact that she was Max's mother and he was all she had left. There was no damn way she was going to let anything happen to him. She headed into the shed and collected her bicycle, hopped on it and pedaled away, passing Jake on the way out.

* * *

Jake ran his hand over the horse's mane. He was beginning to think that moving in with Sara to watch over them was a dumb idea. He was letting his emotions govern his actions and that just wasn't him. What the hell was he thinking moving in? He was single, a damn island in the ocean. He didn't need her. He groaned. For a long time he'd kept his feelings in check but after the event, and all that had happened since, he'd found himself falling into that old pattern of thinking. Falling for a story in which he and she ended up together. It didn't help being around her. Evenings they would drink wine, spend time talking about their younger days and... Ugh, he groaned again, pushing it from his mind. To survive he couldn't become complacent or allow himself to get bogged down by another person.

He watched her in the distance veer around the bend in the road heading south while he went north. The horse broke into a gallop and he shifted his mind to what was before them. Although the town now had forty volunteers helping to keep the peace and it felt relatively safe, he knew that the introduction of FEMA could be both a blessing and a curse. The need was high, that was for sure. But it was mostly for medical supplies. Food and water wasn't an issue as the bay around them offered an abundant amount of fish and they'd already held a meeting in the early months after the event to discuss growing vegetables and helping one another. Teresa used Sara as an example, opening up the inn to those who didn't feel safe. So far only Rita, Tess and the Sterlings had taken her up on the offer. Though safety was found in numbers, giving up a home to live with someone else meant taking on responsibilities and not everyone wanted to pitch in.

When Jake turned onto Court Street, which led to Emerson Hall, he noticed a large military Humvee parked nearby. There were more than the usual number of residents gathered outside. Several looked his way as he got closer. He pulled on the reins to slow the horse and hopped off, leading it through the crowd before handing it off to Lou Peterson, one of the volunteers. Lou led the horse around the back to a makeshift stable that had recently been built while Jake passed by six armed residents posted outside. He gave a nod, and they moved aside to let him in. It felt good to know that they had a strong group of residents who were committed to protecting the town. They operated in shifts with thirty on at any given time, the rest would sleep but could be called upon if and when an issue arose. They had spread them out, posting five at the intersection of Wadsworth Cove Road and Castine Road while the rest patrolled the town. The roadblock at the intersection was to prevent an influx of troublemakers from out of town. They rotated in shifts and for the past month they had seen a decrease in crime. Most of it now was petty.

Jake strolled down the hallway.

They had planned to meet in the back, in a rectangular room with the large boardroom table. When he entered, some were seated, others standing around the walls.

"I don't agree with it," Sam said from his seat as Jake shut the door. All eyes shifted to him.

"Sorry I'm late," he said. In the room were three military officials and a tall, thin guy with a balding head wearing a FEMA label on the front of his suit. Beside them were a handful of strangers. Carl, Sam and several members of the town council were also present.

Teresa eyeballed Jake before the FEMA rep replied. "Deputy, the needs of the country and the county outweigh the needs of the few. If all we do is look after our tiny patch of land, what happens to the young, the elderly, the sick and those who don't have the ability to fish or hunt?"

"We take care of them."

"Right, and that's all we are asking for you to do."

"No, Mr. Harris, you are asking us to go above and beyond the needs of this community."

Harris lifted his nose. "Look, I can appreciate what you have established here. You have set a good example for other towns in Hancock County but what you have here is unique. Many of the towns we have passed through have not rallied together. People have died from starvation."

"Isn't that why you're taking them into the camps, to avoid that?"

"Yes. But that means we have more mouths to feed. Like yourselves we have a limited crew to provide security. I'm sure you already understand that these are dangerous times, deputy. Eighty percent of our efforts go towards security, and dealing with internal issues."

"What, like making people work?" Sam shot back.

"Everyone has to work, deputy. This town is no different."

"Residents weren't forced to work."

"No one is forcing anyone," Harris replied, narrowing his gaze.

Sam ran a hand over his chin. "That's not what I'm hearing. I heard the FEMA camps are no different than the ones they had in the Soviet Union. What were they called? Gulag camps. That's right."

Jake listened to the conversation, intrigued. His eyes washed over the military officials who stood there like statues just waiting for the word. One of them, a large brooding man with buzzed hair, granite chin and blue eyes, leaned forward and whispered into Harris' ear. He nodded.

"Listen. I understand your situation. However we are in the position whereby we can enforce if need be."

"You mean break the Constitution?"

"No, deputy. The Constitution exists because of government and just as it was created by our founding fathers, it can be laid aside by our present government."

"Convenient."

"Deputy, let me put this in a way that you can understand as you seem to be having trouble grasping the gravity of the situation. Castine is a coastal town, and therefore its existence directly impacts those who are inland. I saw the roadblock and Teresa has informed us that you don't allow anyone into this area who is not from the area. So those wishing to fish. What are they meant to do? Go elsewhere?"

"The coastline extends beyond Castine."

"You're right. It does. However if everyone took the same approach, towns like yours would monopolize all of the coast. There are thousands of towns further in that are in desperate need of food. Now you can either be part of the solution or the problem. How would you like to proceed?"

Sam stared back at him and looked at Teresa. "I'm not the one you should be having this conversation with. I don't govern this town."

"No, but you have built a rapport with the people."

"Actually, Jake has," Sam said, glancing over to him.

"It's because of him that we have people patrolling the area and keeping others safe. Now you want us to go out there and tell the residents they need to double the amount of time they spend fishing because FEMA wants them to contribute to the effort?"

"In times of war, everyone must contribute."

"But we are not at war, are we?" He waited for a response, hoping they would shed more light on what caused the EMP. They didn't.

Harris ran his tongue over the front of his teeth. "Again, you have a choice to be the solution or the problem. But let me lay it out for you. Martial law is in effect. We have the right to take firearms, ammunition and supplies. It would be very difficult to protect this town if you didn't have firearms, am I right?"

Carl rose to his feet and stabbed his finger at Harris. "You piece of shit. Are you threatening us?"

"Sit down," the military official said in a booming voice, his hand on his weapon. Carl looked at him and shook his head. "So that's how it's gonna be? Right. I got it."

Harris walked over to a window with his hands clasped behind his back. "Deputies, we are not the enemy here. We want what you want. Freedom. But in order for that to happen we must work together." He turned around and faced them. "Don't make this harder than it needs to be."

Chapter 4

Military? There had to be at least twenty of them. Max and Eddie watched the group stream up the dock, going back and forth from the house to boats to collect supplies. A couple of guys handed off large duffel bags, and big moving boxes. They heard them joking with one another and a couple sprinted toward the house like they were in some race. "They with you?" Eddie asked.

"Does it look like it?" Max shot back as they crouched in a grove of trees. "What the hell is the military doing on this island?"

Eddie fished into his bag and pulled out a pair of binoculars. He played around with the focus. "That's not the military."

"How do you know?"

He tapped his arm. "The patch. That's Maine Militia. It's a very distinct logo. Take a look," he said handing over the binos. Max peered through and focused on the shoulder of one of the men. Sure enough he saw the word Militia. He lowered the binoculars.

"How long have you been coming here?" Max asked.

"A few weeks. At first I went to some of the other islands in the area but this one had alcohol in the house, and well, the infinity pool. Hard to pass that up," he said with a grin.

"And you never saw anyone else?"

"Not until you. Which by the way, might I say you really need to get some sun. I've never seen an ass that white. You're like a damn snowman."

Max looked at him and Eddie laughed. "Look, they would have seen my boat. Where's yours?" Max asked.

"On the east side of the island." He pointed through the heavily wooded area.

Max got up and tapped him on the shoulder. "Well come on, let's get going."

Eddie shrugged. "Why? This place just got interesting."

"Are you kidding me? They're armed."

Eddie raised one of Max's gun magazines. "As are we, my friend."

"Okay, I think you're a little demented, possibly delusional. We need to get off this island before they know we're here. Now let's go."

Eddie grumbled. "Man, you are such a buzz killer."

They took off jogging through the woods, putting as much distance as they could between them and the house. The east and south sides of the island were nothing but woodland. They trudged through with Eddie leading the way. "So you never told me how things have gone for you since the blackout. How is it over in Castine?"

"You haven't been there?" Max asked.

"Hey, I just visit islands that look interesting. I don't want to go where there's people."

"And yet you wanted to hang with those guys back there."

"I wanted to observe. For all we know they might be dropping off supplies." He stopped walking. "Hell, we might have found a gold mine. Think about it. This place is so out of the way. Perhaps they were looking for a spot to leave their firearms, and other goodies." He turned around. "I really think we should go back. Just to see."

"Eddie. No. I value my life a lot more."

"They won't kill us. We're just two teens out exploring."

"Famous last words," Max said trudging past him. "Come on, where is this damn boat?"

He laughed. "They really do have you spooked, don't they? I bet you and your family have been hiding in Castine. Isn't that right?"

Max turned to face him. "Yeah. That's what we do. Hide. We've managed to survive this long by hiding. Idiot!"

"I bet you don't even know how to use that gun, do you?"

Max replied over his shoulder. "Give me one of the magazines, and I'll show you."

That made Eddie snort. As they came out of the tree line, he stopped walking then burst forward looking to the left and right. "Where is it?"

"Hilarious. Let me guess, this is where you tell me you were sure you moored the boat here."

He jabbed his finger towards a tree. "I did, I tied it up right..." Eddie trailed off as he approached the tree and saw the line had been cut. All that was left was a short piece of rope. He looked at the frayed end and then back at Max. Max still thought he was joking until he noticed he wasn't laughing.

"Well, it has to be around here. Where are those binoculars?"

Eddie pulled them out and looked through, scanning the horizon. They wandered further east, strolling around the island. "C'mon! Come on!" he bellowed before Max told him to shut up.

"You want to bring them over here?"

"They can't hear us, numbnuts. The island's too big."

"Not big enough that they wouldn't hear your big mouth!" He glared at him.

Eddie made a gesture to the water. "The boat. It's out

there."

"What?" Max ripped the binos from his hand and took a look. Sure enough, his small fishing boat was between Nautilus and Holbrook Island. "Oh well that is great. Just great. Shit!" he bellowed before realizing he'd just done exactly what he'd reprimanded Eddie for. "We are so screwed."

He dropped to a crouch and ran his hands over his head.

"Look, we can just wait until low tide and then make our way across to Grays Island."

"Eddie. I've lived here long enough to know the tide might get low but not low enough. The bay's water will still be deep."

He waved him off. "No, it would be one or two feet at the most."

"Yeah, and when would that happen?"

"Usually around mid-day."

Max shook his head. "How do you know that?"

"My old man is a fisherman. I've been out with him

enough times to know."

Max looked at his wristwatch, it was just after eight thirty in the morning. He tapped it and showed Eddie. "Three and a half hours. First, even if you're right, that still means we have to stay here until then. Now I don't know about you but I figure that if those guys find my boat, and they cut yours loose, they probably know someone is on the island. In which case they'll find us before mid-day."

"No they won't. I know this island better than them."

"I thought you said you've only been out here a few times."

"Yeah. Well. You can learn a lot about an island when you don't have someone else slowing you down."

Max rose. "Seriously? Let me know if I'm holding you back. I only want to survive."

"And we will. But you need to relax. Geesh, anyone would think you suffer from PTSD."

Max glared at him. "Let's just find somewhere to hide until mid-day."

He nodded and jerked his head. "Follow me. I've got this."

They had turned to wander back up the pebbly beach toward the woodland when they found themselves looking at five guys with rifles aimed at them. Eddie dropped the magazine in his hand. "You were saying," Max replied as his hands slowly went up.

* * *

Ray Ferguson was just getting settled into the new digs when the double doors at the rear of the house burst open and two young guys were thrust in, almost tripping over each other. "Hey, you mind? Fuck! This jacket is worth more than your paycheck. Now can I get my sunglasses back?" the kid with an attitude and a hip-looking army jacket said.

"Roberts. What's this?"

"Found them snooping around on the east side of the island."

"We're weren't snooping, we trying to get off the island," the emo-looking kid added.

"What's your name, kid?" Ray asked the emo.

"Max."

Ray gave a nod toward the other one. "And you?"

"Ask your mother, I banged her last night."

Ray snorted finding him amusing. He was full of spit and vinegar, a lot like him when he was that age. "His name is Eddie," Max said rolling his eyes at him.

"Hey. Don't tell him that," Eddie said, scowling.

Ray went over and walked in front of them like a drill instructor. "You know this is private property. You shouldn't be here."

"Neither should you," Eddie said. He approached Eddie and stared him in the eye. Eddie snorted. "Are you meant to be intimidating?"

Ray smiled. "Anyone else with you?"

"No, it's just us," Max said, dropping his chin.

"Where you from?"

"Castine. And he's…"

"I can talk for myself," Eddie interjected. "I'm from here. My uncle owns this place." Max looked at him. Was this another one of his elaborate stories or was he telling the truth?

"Really? And what's your uncle's name?" Ray asked.

He was quiet then he shot out a name. "Nigel Banning."

"Nigel."

"That's right. And he'll be really pissed when he finds out that you and your goons have—"

"Kid, shut the fuck up. I know the owner of this house. I rented it multiple times over the last few years."

"You can rent this place?" Max asked.

"Oh yeah, it will cost you around twenty-two hundred a night, or twelve grand for a week but it's rentable," Eddie said. Both Max and Ray looked at him. "What? I looked into it. I was thinking of renting it."

"From your uncle?" Ray asked with a smirk.

"Well yeah, him and my old man aren't exactly on the same page. If you know what I mean."

"Shut up." Ray brought a hand up and ran it over his face. "Now, what to do with you two?" He removed his handgun from its holster.

Eddie instantly dropped to his knees with his hands together like he was praying. "Please. I'm too young to die. I'll do anything... well, barring sexual favors, I mean if push comes to shove, I'll go there but I'm really not into all that man sweat, if you know what I mean. Just... please don't kill me." He started sobbing like a small child. Ray looked at him then at Max who looked surprised, maybe even embarrassed by his friend.

Ray chuckled, then started laughing harder. Eddie looked at him and then started laughing too. "Seriously, where did you meet this guy?" he asked Max.

Max thumbed over his shoulder. "By the pool, he stole my clothes."

That only made him laugh harder. "Oh, shit, I like you two. Get up off the floor. I'm not gonna kill you. You should have seen the look on your face. What a pussy." He strolled off. "You guys hungry?"

"Famished," Eddie replied.

"Good." He yelled over his shoulder. "Jackson. Whip

us up some food."

"You got it!" Jackson replied from a different room.

"Get you boys a drink?"

"Beer, if you have it?" Max said.

Ray wagged his finger at him. "That's what I like, someone who knows what he wants." He crossed the room to a small cooler on the floor and took out a beer and tossed it to Max. He caught it and looked at the label. Beads of water dripped off the red Budweiser logo. Max cracked the top and took a swig. It was cold.

"I keep them in bay water. My own personal refrigerator," he said before chuckling.

"Oh, we have actual ice," Max said.

Ray frowned. "Really? You got power?"

Max swallowed a mouthful of beer. "No, Rodney Jennings. A kid on the island. He figured out a way to make ice with water and acetone. Smart as shit. You should see it."

"I'd like that," he said sinking into one of the leather chairs, then pointing. "Take a seat."

Both of them looked at each other then dropped down.

"You guys smoke?"

Max shook his head. "Weed. That's about it."

"Why you offering?" Eddie asked, looking at him for a handout. Ray took out a small tin of cigars and tossed him one along with a box of matches. "So what brought you two out here?"

Max took another swig. "Exploring."

"By the way, did your guys cut my boat loose? On the east side," Eddie asked.

"Probably."

"What about mine?" Max asked. "Down by the dock."

"It's still there. For now. Tell me more about this ice man of yours."

"He's just a resident on the island in Castine. That's where I'm from. I live in the Manor."

"A manor?"

"My parents run an inn over there."

"And what's the situation like? Any military presence?"

"No. But I heard my mother saying something about FEMA coming to town or something like that."

Ray turned and looked at his brother. Lee raised his eyebrows.

"Why? You work with them?" Max asked.

That made him laugh. "No, kid. Unfortunately that boat has sailed."

He took a large hit on his cigar and watched Eddie light his. Eddie started coughing hard. "Wow, those are powerful."

"How old are you two?"

"Seventeen. I turn eighteen in a few months," Eddie said.

"You ever thought of joining the military?" Ray asked. He was always on the lookout for new blood. Before the blackout there were dozens of core members in Waldo County, and many chapters found in thirteen of Maine's sixteen counties. The actual number of militia spread across the different counties varied from year to year. There had been at one point up to 3,500 of them but in this neck of the woods there were only a few hundred. Not all of them were as committed as his group, that's why he only had around thirty men.

Max looked back at him. "Why?"

"Curious. We could always use another two scouts."

"Fuck that. And get shot?" Eddie said.

"For someone that walks around with an army jacket on, you certainly act like a bitch," Ray said. That made Max laugh.

Eddie frowned, pursing his lips. "I was just playing you. You think those were real tears? Man, you are gullible."

Ray laughed.

"How does someone join?" Max asked.

Ray blew out smoke from the corner of his mouth. "Well we usually expect a member to own a rifle with a hundred rounds of ammunition, a backpack with specific gear in it, practice winter camping, know some survival techniques, and…" He started laughing. "Look, we have some formality to go through but I think with you two we could bypass all of that. You know how to shoot a gun?"

"I do," Max said. He looked at Eddie.

"Well obviously. Geesh," Eddie said, taking a large swig of his beer and not looking him in the eye. Cleary he hadn't, but the emo kid — there was potential there.

Chapter 5

Think fast. Beth's heart drummed hard at the sound of a door slamming, and voices echoing in the house. Even if the key to the truck was among the set and she managed to get the vehicle started, the men's truck was blocking the exit. She only had two options: leave by way of the garage door or enter the house and... well, face them. Beth kept a firm grip on Grizzly. "Quiet, boy," she said trying to focus.

"I'm telling you we should have shot him when we had the chance."

"And where would that have got us?" another voice replied. "No, we need them as much as they need us. We play this out for as long as we can. Alliances are important, Ned."

"Bo, I'm not saying they aren't but these trades don't seem fair."

Beth wondered if she just waited in the garage whether

they would leave again. The sound of a portable stove kicking in, and one of them asking the other if he wanted coffee, made it clear they weren't going anywhere. She couldn't take Grizzly out there. His nails tapping on the wooden floor would be a clear giveaway. She had no other choice than to face them. "Wait here. Okay? I'll be back," she said to Grizzly. He let out a soft whine and she glared at him. Sometimes that was all it took for him to understand. He sat down while she approached the door and eased it open. *Don't creak. Don't creak.* She peered down the corridor. A large bearded man walked past the doorway of the kitchen. She pulled back. Damn it. Turning to Grizzly, she brought a finger up to her lips.

Again she looked.

It was all clear.

Pulling her handgun from its holster she stepped out and closed the door behind her. Slowly she inched her way toward the kitchen. Her pulse was racing. She could hear the blood rushing in her ears.

"Horsemeat for ammunition. I think it's worth more. I

think we should be getting far more. That was our last horse. We should have held on to it."

"Ned, you don't get it. Ammunition is a rare commodity right now. People are going through it like wildfire. We can hunt for our food but we can't beat a person to death with a horse."

"You can trample them."

Both of them laughed. "Here, take your coffee and shut up."

"Ah, service with a smile."

Beth rounded the corner to find one of the men seated at a small table in the kitchen with his back turned to her, and the other one leaning against the counter with a cup of coffee close to his lips. They were both rugged in appearance and wearing ratty-looking jeans, work boots and plaid shirts. "Don't move," she said.

"I wasn't planning on it. Coffee?" the one guy standing beside the counter asked gesturing to a French press.

"All I want is the keys to your truck."

"You hear that, Ned? All she wants is the keys."

"Guessing you're Bo?" she said to the one by the counter.

"That's right. Do we know each other?"

"No. Now the keys, please," Beth said, her hand extended.

"You know how many people have walked through our doors asking for the same thing and have left empty-handed? Some never left but that's another story."

She wiggled her fingers. "Keys."

"You won't get far. Trust me. We might not get you but the roads out there are hostile, especially for a pretty girl like you. Now if you need to get somewhere, maybe we can come to some arrangement."

"Just give me the fucking keys before I rearrange your face."

Ned snorted. "Fiery one."

"Yeah, I like that," Bo said. "Tell me, what's the urgency?"

Beth fired a round at the floor and both of them nearly shit bricks. "Your life," she said, then gestured again for the keys. Bo reached into his top shirt pocket and tossed them over. She caught them with her left hand. "Now both of you get on the floor."

They both dropped onto their bellies and Beth reached for what looked like a horse leash hanging on a hook. She tossed it to Ned. "Tie your pal up."

He looked at her with a frown. "You know, you don't need to do this. Not everyone is bad."

"Sorry, can't take a chance."

Ned hogtied Bo, and then dropped down so Beth could move in and do the same with him. "At least let us know why you need it?"

"My friend is injured. I need to get him medical attention."

"Shot?"

"Bitten by a copperhead," she said as she tied Ned up. Strangely he didn't put up a fight, though the gun to the back of his head, and her knee pushed into his shoulder blade, probably helped.

"You need antivenom. Guessing you are heading for

Port Jervis. That's a good twenty-minute ride from here. I figure whoever is bitten can't be far otherwise you wouldn't be risking your neck to try and get medication. Let me save you the hassle. The town is in ruins. Anything that should be operational isn't. Pharmacies and grocery stores have been looted. You'll find yourself stepping over the dead. As for the hospital. No one is there. Now I know a guy who has what you need but that requires you trusting us. But can you do that?"

"I just told you."

"Right. You can't take chances."

Beth jabbed him with a finger. "How about you tell me where this guy of yours is?"

"You won't get to him without us. Trust me on that," Bo said.

She stared at him, fully aware that this could just be some elaborate story to get her to free them, but then on the other hand, if he was telling the truth she could find herself spinning wheels, getting ambushed or worse — not getting back in time to save Landon.

"Ah, let her go," Ned said. "She seems like a big girl who can handle herself. Dixon will love her."

Beth walked out of the room and got Grizzly. When she came back in, they were rolling around trying to get out of their restraints. They took one look at the dog and their eyes widened. "Here's what I'm gonna do. I'll take you with me," she said to Bo. "Your pal here can stay."

"No. If I go, so does he. Sorry, that's a rule we don't break. It's what's kept us alive."

"And yet you're both on the floor right now."

"But still alive," Bo said, a grin forming. He must have seen her hesitation as he continued, "How old are you? Eighteen, nineteen?"

"What's it to you?" she asked.

"I had a daughter about the same age."

She could tell he was trying to engage on some other level but she didn't have time for that. "Look, I have to go. I would love to chit chat but…"

"You have to get the antivenom. Right. Well, I wish you all the best. We could have been of help to you…

and your friend."

Beth exited with Grizzly and loaded him into their truck. It was a 1984 Chevrolet Blazer. She inserted the key and it started without any trouble. Huh. He hadn't lied about that. As she backed out of the driveway she couldn't help but ponder what he'd said. If the town was in bad shape and overrun, the odds of her making it in and out without trouble were slim. Gangs, bandits, troublemakers; they'd hear the vehicle coming. And who was this Dixon? She sighed and slammed on the brakes. The truck idled at the mouth of the driveway as she stared at the house. "Damn it!" she said smacking her hand against the steering wheel.

The what-ifs bombarded her mind.

What if he was right?

What if the town was overrun?

What if she got grabbed by a large group?

What if, what if?

Everything told her to take a risk but was that the smart thing to do? Twenty minutes. She could reach Port

Jervis in twenty minutes. She looked at the fuel gauge which was almost full. If he was wrong she could return and… What was she thinking? The clock was ticking. Every second she wasted was one step closer to Landon losing a limb, or losing his life. Beth hopped out of the truck and went back into the house. She opened the door and went over to Bo and cut his legs free but not his wrists which were still behind his back. "You're coming with me."

"I told you. I don't—"

"So is he," she said. She forced him outside, over to the truck and loaded him in the back near Grizzly. "Grizzly. Keep an eye on him." The dog turned and snarled as she returned to collect Ned. He was still trying to get his hands free even as she cut his restraints and pushed him out the door. "Look, I get you don't like me. I wouldn't either. But I'll be out of your hair really quick." She thrust him into the drivers side while she rode shotgun. "Here's how this is going to play out. You will take me to your friend. If he doesn't exist, I will shoot you both. If you lead me into any trap, I will shoot you both. If you even attempt to overpower me, I will—"

"Shoot us both. I think we get it," Ned said.

Ned spun the wheel and they roared out onto the open road heading north.

"Where we heading?" Beth asked.

"There is a Methodist church on the left, we have to turn onto Greenville Turnpike and keep going until Old Mountain Road, then we'll swing a right," Bo said. She glanced at them. Grizzly kept baring his teeth.

"This dog of yours isn't too friendly."

"He has a sense for people."

"Well maybe you can put in a good word for us," Bo said.

They kept on driving and Beth took in the familiar sight of vehicles stranded on the road, and homes that were burned. Some had windows smashed and there were a few bodies on the lawns. "You two own that horse training facility back there?" she asked.

"Me and my brother did," Bo replied. "What about

yourself? Where are you from?"

"North Carolina."

"That's quite the distance. Were you vacationing out here when the blackout happened?"

She wasn't sure how much to tell them so she just lied. "Yeah. Visiting friends."

Bo nodded, keeping his eyes on her. It was a little off-putting. She considered herself a fairly good judge of character but with everyone on the defensive it was hard to tell who was good or bad. "So you're heading back there?"

"Yes." She lied again because after the incident with Ruby she didn't want anyone knowing where they were going. Landon had made that mistake. She wouldn't.

"Where's your friend?" Ned asked.

"Doesn't matter," she replied as they pulled onto Old Mountain Road. "Where now?"

"I told you. We keep going for a few miles and there is a dirt road on the right."

Bo interjected. "Ned, keep an eye out for the orange

sign otherwise you'll blow past it."

"I know."

"Where does it go?" Beth asked.

"It leads down to a junkyard." Beth focused on the road until she saw the orange sign. They veered off and the truck bounced up and down. The potholes were huge.

"God, I hate this road. I wish he would fill it in," Ned said.

"What's your friend's name?"

"Horace, but you better leave the talking to me. He's a little high-strung," Bo replied.

"Oh he's high all right," Ned said before chuckling.

The road snaked into a dense green woodland until it came to a rusted ten-foot gate with barbed wire curled around the top. There were multiple red and white signs that read: *Private Property No Trespassing* and *This Property Is Protected by Video Surveillance* and *Violators Will Be Shot.* Ned eased off the gas and brought the truck to a stop. He killed the engine and Beth took the keys and got out and opened Bo's door. She strong-armed him out and stood behind him pressing her handgun into the small of his back. "Well get him out here."

"It doesn't exactly work like that."

Through the gates Beth could see a dilapidated trailer, a run-down office building and hundreds of vehicles stacked on top of one another. "Remember. You lie to me—"

"And you shoot me. I got it. Man, this event really has got you rattled."

"Horace!" Bo yelled. "It's me. Bo. You there?"

There was no answer. No movement. With no power the video cameras didn't move. Bo tried yelling his name again but got no response. Beth glanced back at Ned.

"Perhaps he's dead," she said.

Bo laughed. "Dead drunk, maybe, but not dead. This guy will outlive us all."

Bo continued to call out but after getting no response, Beth was beginning to think they were lying. She pushed Bo toward the gate and checked the lock which connected with a thick chain. She rattled it. No one was getting through that even if they had bolt cutters. Either side of the gate was a chain-link fence that went around the property.

Just as they were about to see if there was another way in, a window on the trailer door dropped and the muzzle of a gun emerged. "Who's that with you?"

"A friend."

"Oh yeah, how about your friend step away from you?"

"Can't do that!" Beth yelled.

"You asshole. Why did you bring trouble my way?"

"She's not trouble."

Beth pushed the gun harder into his back. "You sure?"

"I'm trying to help you here," he said in a low voice before continuing to address Horace. "Listen. All I need is some snake antivenom. For a copperhead. You've got that, right?"

"Who's hurt?"

"Shit, Horace. Would you just open the gates?"

"What you got to trade?"

"You never said anything about trading," Beth muttered.

Bo replied. "Nothing is for free. You got anything?"

"No."

"Well he isn't going to give it away. So here's my suggestion. You give him that bow of yours."

"I'm not handing that over."

"Then the gun."

"Do you think I'm stupid?" Beth replied.

"Hey look, it's your friend's life. The sooner you get that, the better, right?"

Beth rolled her lower lip into her mouth and tapped her foot. She pulled him back to the truck and looked in the rear. "I'm telling you. He's not interested in much except weapons and…" Bo trailed off.

"What?"

"Well you know. He likes his women."

"And you had an eighteen-year-old daughter?"

"Hey, I'm not suggesting that. I'm just saying what he likes. There isn't much wiggle room, if you get my drift."

Beth stared through the fence. "Tell him I'll give him this handgun."

"That's more like it. Horace! We got a…" He turned back to her. "What is that?"

"SIG SAUER."

Bo shouted out the model.

"It got ammo?"

Beth nodded.

"Yep," Bo replied.

The door on the trailer burst open and out came this old guy wearing nothing more than a pair of pee-stained white Y-fronts, a pair of flip flops and a bathrobe. His hair was a shocking white and he had a patch covering one eye. He looked off to his left and right before hurrying towards the gate and unlocking it. "Make it quick."

Beth put Bo back in the truck and Ned drove them in. The old man closed the gate behind them and locked it. A feeling that she was being led like a lamb to the slaughter came over her. She parked and went to get out to find the old man peering through the window at her, his gun at the ready. "You want to tell your buddy to back up," Beth said.

"You want to cut me loose," Bo said twisting in his seat. She reached over and cut his wrist restraint, and he got out.

"What about me?" Ned asked.

"You're staying put," she said as she hopped out only to have the old man nudge her towards the trailer.

"Go on in," Horace demanded.

Beth hesitated.

"You should do as he says. He gets a little agitated when people don't listen," Bo said.

Beth nodded and headed into the trailer. Inside she was greeted by a funky smell of bad body odor, cigarettes and piss. It was truly awful. There was a small table covered in all manner of crap from unwashed plates to cups with coffee stains and dead flowers in a vase at the center. An old radio crackled in the background. It was like an RV but one that had been abused badly. The seating was torn up and faded, the ceiling yellow from smoke and the flooring warped with water stains. Horace shut the door behind him. He shuffled over to his table and took a spoonful of fermented cabbage and downed it before letting out a fart and scratching his ass.

"Well, let's see the goods then."

Chapter 6

It was complete hell. It felt like someone had doused his body in gasoline and set it on fire. Landon's arm had swollen considerably. His vision kept blurring. As hard as he tried to remain calm, he was on the verge of panicking. He writhed in agony as Billy sat across from him strumming his banjo like he didn't have a care in the world. He almost looked as if he was enjoying watching Landon suffer.

Landon looked at his wristwatch again.

Seconds seemed like hours as he waited for Beth to return. He'd tried to meditate to shift his mind away from the pain but it was unbearable. The portion of his hand that had been bitten was already beginning to look darker than the rest of the surrounding skin. Billy said it was tissue damage.

Landon looked his way. He had questions, lots of them. Billy had been good at dodging questions since joining them but there was something that had been niggling Landon since Pennsylvania. They'd stopped in the town of Boiling Springs to replenish some of their supplies and Billy had been less than enthusiastic to stay there. He'd told him he'd meet them on the trail farther up, but when they said they were planning to stay an extra night, it was like a switch flipped in his head. He began acting erratic, saying they were selfish and that if it wasn't for him they would probably be dead. Landon wanted answers but he refused to say why he wouldn't go into town. It wasn't the first red flag, there were others, like finding IDs in his backpack that didn't belong to him. He said they were from his hiking group that had been murdered and he wanted to return to them to the families but Landon didn't buy that. There was something very off about him. Any time they tried to discuss what happened at his camp and how that one man had managed to kill his friends, he would just close up, walk away or retire for the evening.

Boiling Springs was another strange one.

Landon had been approached by a guy who told him not to trust Maestro but before he could explain, Billy stabbed him then justified it by saying that he was trying to lure them into a trap. Beth had bought it as they barely got out of that town with their lives but something didn't ring true.

"That guy in Boiling Springs. The one you stabbed."

"What about him?" Billy said between strums.

"I got a sense he knew you. Had you ever seen him before?"

"Nope."

"Strange. As he knew your trail name."

Billy's eyes lifted and then he chuckled. "You know how many times I've been on this trail?" He waited for Landon to shake his head. "Six times. Back and forth I have hiked this trail. How many times have you?"

"This is the first."

"Exactly. That's why you wouldn't know. You see, even though the hiking community is spread out across the country, there is only a core group of people who hike for the love of it. They're not out here trying to look the part, or fill up their Instagram with shots of the outdoors. They're here because they truly love hiking. In that small community, people know my name because I have hiked every major trail across the United States." He took a deep breath. "John Muir, Continental Divide, Appalachian, Long Trail, Hayduke, Grand Enchantment, Ozark Highlands, Ice Age and Superior. You name it, I have done it more than twice. So my name is out there in the forums. People see me on a regular basis. Of course that guy knows me."

Landon hesitated before he said, "Then why did he warn me about you?"

That made him stop strumming. He set his banjo down beside him. Landon gripped his handgun tighter. "Because people are jealous."

"Jealous?"

He nodded. "That's right. You might think hikers don't get jealous but they are some of the most jealous people in the world. They live for the feedback from others. Oh, you hiked that trail? Oh, you did it without assistance, oh, you hiked with an ultralight backpack... the list goes on."

"Jealousy is one thing. Saying someone is dangerous is another," Landon said.

Billy didn't look fazed by his response. "Look, bad shit happens out here. I've seen it all. People love to point the finger. Blame. Accuse. But that's all it is. If I was you I wouldn't think too much about it. You don't want to go down that rabbit hole."

He got up and took out a pack of cigarettes. There were none left. "Fuck!" he said before crumpling the packet and tossing it. He looked at Landon and sneered before he stepped out of the shelter.

"Where you going?"

"To get some air."

He disappeared around the corner and Landon glanced at his watch again. "C'mon, Beth. Where are you?"

* * *

Beth handed over the gun and Horace pulled out the magazine and looked at her. "And the rest?" She took out the spare magazines from her backpack and slapped them down on the grimy counter. He took them and disappeared into the back where they could see him opening a safe and putting them inside. He came out and went over to a cooler and took out a beer, cracked the top off and chugged some of it down.

"The antivenom?" Beth asked.

"All in good time. Take a seat."

"Look, I need to get back and fast."

"Take a seat!" he bellowed. Beth looked at Bo and he nodded. Beth glanced at the clock on the wall. There was still time.

"And you," Horace said to Bo. "Dixon came snooping around here yesterday. Said you're screwing him over."

Bo chuckled. "He thinks everyone screws him over. I gave him a good deal."

Horace went to the counter and opened a tin full of tobacco and began to roll himself a cigarette. He licked the ends of the cigarette paper in a disgusting manner while eyeing Beth. "You're pretty. A lot prettier than the ones he usually brings."

Beth frowned and her gaze bounced to Bo. Bo wouldn't look at her.

Horace laughed. "You didn't tell her?"

Beth's hand slowly dropped to her left leg. She unclipped the sheath that held her knife and wrapped her fingers around it.

"How old are you?" he asked.

"Young enough to be your granddaughter," she said.

He used the tip of his tongue to pry loose a piece of meat stuck between his teeth. "Stand up and turn around."

"Why?"

"Because you want antivenom and that costs more than a handgun is worth."

"What the hell are you talking about? We had a deal."

"A deal?" Horace said, his hand resting on the sawed-off shotgun. "I didn't say anything about a deal. Did I,

Bo?"

Bo shook his head, still refusing to make eye contact with Beth. That bastard. He'd screwed her over. Her hand gripped tightly on the knife. "Dixon has a lot of men that need to be taken care of. You look like you fit the bill but I need to take some measurements. You understand?"

When she didn't respond fast enough, Horace brought the shotgun up. "And I'll take that bow of yours, and that knife you have your hand on. Slowly," he said. Beth felt like such a fool. She shouldn't have trusted him. But she wasn't ready to hand over everything, not without a fight.

"I'll hand it over when I see the antivenom."

"Girl, don't be cute with me. Throw the bow and knife over here."

She gritted her teeth and removed the bow and tossed it near his feet along with the quiver of arrows. Then she removed the knife. "Careful. Nice and slow," he said. She dropped it, though nearer to her than him.

"Really?" he asked. "Kick it over."

She gave it a nudge but not hard.

"More!"

She gave it a harder kick, this time it slipped across the vinyl flooring and under the stove. Horace moved forward but kept the shotgun on her. "Bo. Get it." He then smiled flashing his smoke-stained teeth. "Little girl, you must think I'm stupid," he said. "Come on, Bo. Get the knife or I'll inform Dixon and you know he won't be happy."

Bo got down on his knees and felt around until he had the knife. Horace's eyes were fixed on Beth as Bo suddenly lashed out, jamming the knife into the old man's rib cage and plowing into him. The shotgun went off, blowing a hole through the side of the trailer, and Beth watched as Bo stabbed the guy multiple times until he was no longer moving. When he extracted the blade, he got up and handed it back to her without saying a word. He then strode down the center aisle toward the safe. Beth scooped up her bow and quiver and put it back on. She wiped blood from the knife and put it back in its sheath. All the while Bo was on one knee turning the dial on the front of the safe.

A few seconds later it cracked open and he removed the handgun and magazines along with a small black bag. He unzipped it and looked inside, then closed it and came out. "This is what you need. And here's your gun."

"Why are you helping me?" Beth asked.

"Like I said. Not everyone is bad. We should go."

Beth took her gun and headed out into the bright daylight. When Bo stepped out, he went over to a BBQ and unscrewed the propane tank and lobbed it into the trailer. He then went over to a black truck that was parked nearby and opened up the back and took out multiple cans of gasoline. He went back into the trailer and she could hear liquid splashing and then he came out creating a trail.

"Go. Get in the truck," he said. He dropped the gasoline can, took out of his pocket a lighter and lit it, then tossed it on the ground. A blue flame burst to life and began spreading along the trail of gasoline. Bo turned and bolted for the truck. He hopped in and Beth reversed out at a high rate of speed just as an explosion erupted. Thick black smoke curled up into the air as she spun the wheel and drove away.

"Are you out of your goddamn mind?" Ned said. "Dixon will go nuts."

"He won't know."

"After this morning's fiasco, of course he will."

"The old man got what was coming to him. Sick fuck."

Ned shook his head. "Bo."

"He would have handed her over to him."

"And? How's that any different than the others?"

"Others? What others?" Beth asked. She glared in her rearview mirror at Bo who looked embarrassed to say.

"You don't want to know."

She scoffed. "I think I already do." She shook her head.

"You know he'll kill her now. You just killed Iris."

"No he won't. She means too much to him. Besides,

this could have been anyone."

Ned shook his head. "C'mon, Bo. How many have managed to get into Horace's yard since this shit storm? He's gonna know it was us."

"Yeah, well by then we'll have Iris out."

"And how do you plan on doing that?"

Bo shook his head. "I don't know. I just know that this was the right thing to do."

"For who, her? Because you have just signed our death warrant."

Beth didn't have to think too hard to grasp what they might be referring to and who Dixon could be. After running into Lilith and Bosley, and encountering another crazy group in Boiling Springs, it was becoming the norm to find small groups running towns. Trading, working with neighbors and helping others only got people so far. Eventually people would realize that to monopolize the game, they had to be the one in control before someone else took the reins. "Ned, just shut up. I'm not leaving without her."

"You don't get it, do you? She wants to be with him. Iris chose to be with him. You saw the way she was. You had your chance."

Bo lowered his chin.

"Iris. Is that your daughter?" Beth asked.

He gave a nod.

"Who is Dixon?"

"You don't want to know."

Not everyone could be helped.

But it was clear that people would go to great lengths for family.

Up until that point Beth hadn't cared whether they lived or died but anyone who was willing to get between her and a gun earned her respect, regardless of what they had done. In her side mirror she saw smoke rising high above the trees.

It didn't take them long to get back to Bo's home. When they arrived, Ned charged into the house slamming the door behind him without saying goodbye. Bo sighed and looked at her. "You take care of yourself."

"Will you be all right?" Beth asked.

"We've survived this long. Ned will get over it."

She smiled back. "Listen, I really appreciate what you did back there. In fact, I'm grateful for everything you've done and I kind of feel bad that…"

"Beth. Don't sweat it. Get moving. And be sure to avoid Port Jervis. Things are going to get heated over there real soon." She wanted to tell him where they were going but it was safer not to. She extended her hand and he managed to crack a smile as he shook it. She tossed him the keys. "Again, thanks." Bo gave a nod and she motioned for Grizzly to follow as she took off across the field heading for the woods. She only hoped she wasn't too late. When she reached the tree line she looked back. Bo was no longer outside. He was right. Not everyone was bad. There were still good people out there. Fighting. Struggling to survive. Caught up in seemingly impossible situations. She had no idea what they had got themselves involved in, but she had a sense that whatever it was, it ended today.

Chapter 7

Thirty minutes. The response to antivenom was dramatic and fast. It felt like he'd been rescued by an angel. Beth told him that it could take up to a few hours to feel anything but he already felt improvement within the first fifteen minutes. "We need to get some fluids into you," she said. "Usually, hospitals will hook a patient up to an IV and closely monitor them, and in most cases release them from hospital within six hours, however it could be longer depending on the venom's toxicity, and the person."

"You made it back fast," Billy said, leaning up against the shelter wall with his arms crossed. Beth glanced his way. Unlike Landon he didn't look too enthusiastic about her return, if Landon wasn't mistaken, he looked surprised. "So you didn't encounter any problems?"

"A few but nothing I couldn't handle."

"Interesting." Billy studied Landon.

"We'll stay here the night and by morning you should be good to go," Beth said. "I'll see if I can find us some food."

"I'll come with you," Billy said.

She lifted a hand. "No. I should be fine."

"Ah, I insist. You've done a lot already. Let me carry some of the weight. Besides, I'd be interested in seeing you use that bow of yours."

Landon didn't like it one bit. Billy still hadn't given him a straight answer regarding Boiling Springs. He was beginning to think he was holding back, but why?

"Will you watch over Grizzly?" Beth asked.

"Sure," Landon said. As they walked off towards the tree line, Billy cast a glance his way and Landon felt a sinking feeling in his stomach. Out of view, he slapped away the negative thoughts. It wouldn't do him any good. Instead, he closed his eyes to rest and stroked Grizzly who had curled up beside him.

* * *

At some point he drifted off as when he awoke, it was

pitch dark. Grizzly was whining. He groaned and rolled over wiping drool from his lips. The pain in his hand and arm had subsided considerably. Compared to that morning, he almost felt like it had never occurred. He sat up and rolled his head around. That's when he noticed he was alone. There was no fire and Beth's sleeping bag was still there. "Beth?"

Landon climbed out of his sleeping bag and stumbled out into the campsite. "Billy? Beth?" No answer. He glanced down at his wristwatch and pressed the button on the side to illuminate it. It was after eight at night. He'd been asleep for over nine hours. Where the hell was she? She should have been back by now. He went into the shelter and felt around for his flashlight. He shone it at her spot and then over to where Billy had been. His gear was gone. He tried to recall if he'd left with it but couldn't remember. A sense of dread washed over him. "Beth!" he yelled loudly. Grizzly followed him out into the clearing as he called out to her again but got no reply. No, no, no. This wasn't good. His mind immediately went to the worst scenario. Had they been jumped? Been attacked by an animal? Or was Billy behind it?

Being stranded in the wilderness was hard enough with Beth but on his own? There was no way he would survive out here. He relied on her. She was his lifeline, his anchor in foreign territory. Up in the sky it would have been a different case but down here... in the middle of a forest...panic rose in his chest.

"Beth!"

Convinced she would have been back by now, he hurried over to the shelter and reached into his bag. He pulled out a piece of black charcoal and scribbled on the wood a message for her just in case she returned. There was still a slim possibility that she was still hunting as she had often disappeared for hours when he was at the cabin, but this didn't feel right. He rolled up his sleeping bag and tucked it back into the loops below his backpack, then he guzzled down some water and shrugged on the pack. He checked how much ammo he had left in his magazine before gesturing for Grizzly to follow.

He took Beth's sleeping bag and brought it up to Grizzly's snout.

"Okay, boy, I'm gonna need your help to find her. Can you do that? Find Beth."

Landon wasn't sure it would work but when Grizzly turned and headed for the same area he'd last seen Beth, hope rose inside him.

He tapped on the flashlight and shone it ahead, trudging forward in fear and trepidation. He didn't want to get bitten again, and he didn't want to get attacked by a cougar. The way he saw it, he was smack bang in the middle of the wilderness and anything could happen, especially at night.

* * *

Beth returned to awareness through a hazy fog with a pounding headache. Her eyes blinked a few times. Darkness. The strong smell of the forest and a fire. "Landon?"

A low voice, definitely not Landon's, replied. "Don't try to get up."

A flash of fragmented memories. Walking the trail. Firing an arrow at a rabbit... Turning to say something... then a hard whack on the back of her head. She'd fallen and felt another hard hit to the back of her skull before she went unconscious.

Beth looked towards the flickering fire and the figure sitting on a log beyond it. *Billy.* She tried to move but her wrists were bound tight, as were her ankles. "What the hell are you playing at?"

Billy pulled meat off a bone and chewed. He wagged the bone at her. "This rabbit is good. You hungry?"

She wriggled. "Let me out of these."

"Now now, calm down. I'll release you when you can be trusted."

"Trusted? You piece of shit. Why are you doing this?"

"Because I can."

His response made no sense.

"We helped you."

"That you did, however, all good things must come to an end. Besides, Landon was asking too many questions.

Now in days gone by, I would have just shot you both and continued on, and I could have done that. I mean, not to you but with Landon, but I thought that copperhead would deal with him. But then you went and got the antivenom and well, I knew he would be up on his feet in no time. I couldn't have that so I decided to change things up."

"You bastard."

"Careful. It doesn't take much to change my mind."

"That man Landon shot. He was innocent, wasn't he?"

"Innocent. Who is really innocent, huh?"

"You killed those campers, didn't you? You weren't with any group."

"I was with a group," he shot back, a look of disgust masking his face.

She struggled to sit upright and managed to press her back against a tree. "Why? Why did you kill them?"

He snorted, taking another bite of his food. "Does it matter? Why did you kill people? We all make decisions. Survival is as much about being preemptive as it is staying clear of trouble and dealing with it when it shows up. If anyone should know that, you should. But let's not talk about that, shall we?"

He got up and walked over and crouched in front of her. The flickers of light from the fire created shadows that danced on his face making him seem human for one second, and a devil the next. He brought the leg of the rabbit up to her mouth. "Go on. Eat. You'll need it. We have a long way to go."

She turned her face. He grabbed her by the nose and squeezed it tight forcing her to open her mouth, then inserted the rabbit leg and told her to bite down and swallow or he would jam it down her throat, bone and all. Reluctantly she ripped off a piece of flesh and chewed it a few times.

He smiled. "That's it."

Beth spat it in his face and he instantly lashed out and struck her across the cheek with the back of his hand. "You better start treating me with a little respect otherwise you're gonna wish you died back in North

Carolina."

He got up and walked back to his spot on a log. He took a swig of water, another bite of meat and then tossed the bone into the fire.

She studied him. "What have you done to him?"

"Landon?"

She gave a nod.

"Nothing. I left him there. You should be grateful. I considered going back and strangling him but I figure a man like him won't last long out here. And your dog. Well, he's better off without you."

"Who are you?"

He stopped chewing and chuckled. "I told you. That part I didn't lie about."

"Why are you keeping me alive?"

"I've asked myself that countless times over the past month. I'm not sure. Maybe tomorrow I will change my mind and dump your body in the forest for the cougars to gnaw on. Would you like that?" His lip curled and he got this glint in his eye.

He was clearly insane.

"Now we only have one sleeping bag so you'll be sharing it with me."

She shook her head. "Just kill me now."

He chuckled. "You're the first one who's ever said that."

"The first?"

He stopped eating and got this frown on this face. "Well, I guess to be fair, you're not the first, so to speak. There was a hiker in Pennsylvania who begged me to put her out of her misery." He continued eating as if it didn't faze him. "You'd be surprised at people's last requests." He pulled out some rope. "I used this. I could have used a gun but that's too quick. I killed a few with gasoline but there is nothing like rope. It's just full of possibilities." He slipped the rope back into his pocket.

"You're an animal."

"Of course I am. We are all animals, Beth. It's just we've become civilized. Our pens are homes, our jungle is society and our masters are anyone who we allow to govern our actions. I choose to live as I wish. A bit like your father. I think him and I are alike."

"You are nothing like my father. You're a sorry excuse for a man. One of these days you'll get what's coming to you."

"Yeah?" He stopped eating and walked over to her. She didn't cower back or flinch. A man like him would have liked that. No, if she was going to die by his hand, she'd make damn sure he knew she wasn't afraid. The truth was, she wasn't terrified. Death would have been a sweet escape from the horrors of this world. He unsheathed a knife and brought it up to her neck, pushing the blade slowly against her skin. "Maybe you'll get what's coming to you," he said. "Perhaps I will—"

The crack of a branch, the trudging of feet.

Billy whipped his head around to see who it was. Before she could scream, he shoved a bandanna into her mouth, then placed his hand over her lips. Her muffled cries were barely audible.

"Stay quiet," he said as he blasted away from her and

disappeared into the surrounding forest. Beth tried to push the bandanna out of her mouth with her tongue but he'd shoved it so far back down her throat it was virtually impossible. She began to choke, tears welling up in her eyes as she gagged.

* * *

The glow of a nearby fire illuminated the woods. Although Landon couldn't be sure it was them, he crouched down beside Grizzly and told him to sit and wait. "Don't move, boy." He got up and darted from one tree to the next, his handgun at the ready. Only the crackling and popping of wood could be heard. Landon squinted into the dark. As his eyes adjusted to the light from the firepit, he saw a figure curled over near a tree. He immediately recognized the jacket. *Beth.* Hurrying forward, Landon scanned the camp. It was just her. *Where are you?* Even though he couldn't prove at this point that Billy was behind it, his gut told him otherwise. Wasting no time, Landon rushed into the camp and made his way over to her, all the while looking to his left and right. He even glanced upward. No one. Beth's eyes bulged as he pulled the rag from her mouth and she gasped, taking in air. He began untying her hands as he peppered her with questions.

"Who did this?"

"Billy."

"Where is he?"

Before she had time to answer he heard movement over his shoulder. He shifted just in time as a blade scythed the air near his head. A sharp kick from Billy knocked his gun out of his hand. "Argggh!" Billy yelled as he unleashed his attack. Landon stumbled and Billy dove on top of him. They rolled multiple times, getting closer to the fire. Landon had hold of his wrists. His face twisted as he pressed down the knife, getting it closer and closer to Landon's face.

"Grizzly!" Landon yelled.

Like a bolt of lightning, Grizzly came bounding into the clearing and without even being told what he needed to do, he leapt at Billy, knocking him off Landon. To avoid the dog getting hurt, Landon kept hold of Billy's knife hand, and scrambled on top of him. A quick shift in position, and he now had the upper hand. Grizzly bit down on Billy's pant leg and shook it violently, causing him to scream in pain. Landon drove his forehead into the bridge of Billy's nose, bursting it wide open. He could see his handgun a short distance away but it was too risky. If he let his hand go for even a second it could be fatal. Instead, he drove his knee hard into Billy's nuts and then slammed his knife hand against the ground, hoping to get him to release it.

The assault lasted a few minutes but eventually, Billy released it.

Reach for the knife or gun?

It was a no-brainer. Go for what's closest.

Landon let go of his wrist and lunged for the knife.

But Billy wasn't going down that easy. He bucked him off, kicked the dog in the face with his other foot and scrambled away. By the time Landon was up with the knife in hand, Billy had darted into the forest.

Landon was about to sprint after him when Beth stopped him.

"Landon, no! Let him go. It's too dangerous."

He squinted into the darkness, hearing Billy scamper away.

He retrieved his handgun and cut Beth's restraints. As soon as they were free she wrapped her arms around him. All the while, Landon kept scanning the tree line expecting Billy to appear at any second.

Chapter 8

The discussion around supper that night was heated. From the recent discovery of what FEMA had planned to the disappearance of Max, everyone looked one step away from snapping. After searching for Max all day, Sara was at her wits' end and sick with worry. Even though Rita and Janice had been kind enough to get food together that evening, she wasn't hungry. Sara picked at her fish with a fork while Sam, Carl and Jake argued over the way forward. Their voices got louder the more alcohol they consumed.

"I say we do nothing. What can they do?" Jake said. "Force us to fish for them?"

Sam chimed in. "You heard what Harris said. They'll take our firearms and supplies."

"I'd like to see them try," Carl said.

"So we bury them," Jake said. "We should have done that already by now. With so many homes being broken into and broad daylight thefts, it's only a matter of time before someone targets the inn."

"Did you see the way that colonel put his hand on his gun?" Carl asked.

"It's just a scare tactic," Jake replied, before taking another sip of his wine. "He wouldn't have done anything."

"Before the blackout, maybe not, because there was media. But now? This is the wild west. Anything goes. No one exists to hold them accountable."

Jake shook his head. "The community would rise up against that form of tyranny."

"The community?" Carl said. "Come on. This community has their head in the sand. Half of them have left and willingly handed themselves over to FEMA. They are probably digging ditches as we speak. The other half thinks the lights are coming back on. We only have a small group that might be willing to do something."

"Well, we will see tomorrow, won't we?" Sam said.

Jake continued. "I say we don't wait until tomorrow;

we act now. Take some of our firearms and store them in PVC pipe and bury them along with ammo."

"No. I think the way forward is to work with them," Sam said.

Carl nearly choked on his wine. "You were the one who opposed the idea," Carl was quick to say. He tossed his fork down and then wiped his lips with a napkin.

"Right now we don't have any other option. You want to go up against the U.S. military?" Sam asked.

"You make it sound like they have the entire army. Come on, man. These fools probably have twenty, thirty officers in Bangor. If that."

"Maybe we should go and find out," Sam added.

"What?" Jake asked. "You want to do surveillance on the FEMA camp?"

"For all we know things might be fine there. Maybe the rumors are just bullshit about forced labor."

Carl laughed. "Seriously, Sam. I wonder about you some days. One minute you are against them, the next you are for them."

"I didn't say I was for them."

"WOULD YOU SHUT UP!" Sara bellowed as she slammed her open hand against the table, unable to take any more. Everyone at the table gawked at her in total surprise. It went completely against who she was and how she usually acted. She apologized and got up and walked into the kitchen. Tess glanced at the others then followed her.

"Sara."

"I'm sorry. I just… Max is still not back and they are talking about everything but where he is. That is my number one priority right now."

Tess nodded. "We understand, hon." She looked back into the dining room. The conversation had started again but quieter. "They get it but there is nothing we can do right now. Tomorrow we'll talk with the rest of the group that helped locate the women. Maybe they can…"

"He's not dead!" she shot back.

"I didn't mean to suggest he is but…"

Right then a door slammed and hope sprang up in

Sara's heart. She ducked out into the corridor just in time to see Max heading up the stairs. "Max! Where the hell have you been?"

"Out," he said, continuing to trudge up the steps as if he was allowed to come and go as he pleased. She hurried to the bottom of the steps. "Young man. Get down here now." He stopped climbing the stairs and looked back at her.

"What?"

"Don't what me. I have been going out of my mind with worry. Do you know I spent the entire day looking for you? That's right. We were this close to calling out a search party," she said holding up her thumb and index finger. "Now where have you been?"

"I went fishing."

"Fishing?"

"Yeah. I never used to need permission to do that."

"We weren't facing the situation we are now. That changes everything."

"Yeah it has. People have just become bigger dicks," he

said heading back up the stairs.

Sara bristled. "What? What did you say? Are you referring to me? Young man."

"Oh God, man, what?" he said turning at the top of the stairs. "I'm tired. I want to go to bed."

"You don't just get to come and go as you please."

"I'm seventeen."

"Until you are eighteen and while you are living under this roof you will abide by the rules. You hear me?"

"Then maybe it's time I moved out." He continued walking out of her line of sight. Now under any other conditions she might have let that go and dealt with it in the morning, especially since they had guests, but she was damned if she was going to let her kid speak to her like that. Sara dashed up the stairs nearly tripping in the process. Tess tried to get her to leave it but she wouldn't. She charged into his room, swinging the door open and slamming it behind her. Max's eyes widened as he pressed his back into the corner of the room. "Mom. Do you mind?"

She wagged a finger in his face. "I mind that you left without telling me where you were going. I mind that you exited through the window because you knew what I would say. I mind that you strolled in acting like you can do whatever the hell you want! And I mind when you refer to me as a dick!"

"I wasn't referring to you."

"Don't bullshit me."

The door opened behind her and Sam walked in. "Sara. How about you go down and have a cup of tea. This is getting a little out of hand."

She turned. "Don't tell me what to do in my own house."

He raised both hands defensively. "You're not thinking clearly."

Max nodded. "Yeah, Mom, you're not…"

She glared at Max and he went quiet. Her jaw was clenched. She hadn't been this angry in a long time. She rarely shouted at her kids and never once had she raised a hand to them. Overall they were good kids. They had been lucky in that regard. While her parents had spanked her as a child, she'd always thought that kids didn't need to be spanked if they were raised correctly, and after both of her kids reached their teens without issue, she had proven that theory correct. But now she could see why some parents went over the edge. Max was right in saying that he'd never had to ask for permission to go fishing but that was before the blackout, before the attack on their home, before the murders in town. She was scared and had good reason. The world around them had changed and they no longer knew who to trust. Ian was a good example of that. She didn't even want to imagine what might have happened had he accepted the invitation to stay at the inn.

She jabbed a finger at Max. "We are not done."

With that she turned and prodded Sam's chest indicating for him to step out of the room. Once they were out on the landing, she closed the door so Max couldn't hear them. "I don't appreciate you telling me what to do in front of my son."

"I'm still a police officer and…"

"And a guest in my house. Don't forget that."

Sam took a deep breath. "I'm sorry. It's just you look exhausted. I know when I'm like that I will bite the head off anyone that comes near me. We're all a bit fired up right now and you have every right as a mother to be upset. But you said the reason you allow people to stay here is so we could support one another. This is me trying to support you."

Sara closed her eyes and tried to get her heart to stop thumping. She nodded. "I'm sorry. I shouldn't have snapped. You're right. I need sleep."

"Why don't you get an early night? We'll clean up and I'll have a word with Max."

She pursed her lips and gave a strained smile before brushing past him and heading for her room. She knew he was right. Tiredness brought out the worst in her, it amplified the small annoyances. She headed off to her room hoping she'd feel better by the morning. At the bottom of the stairs, Tess and Jake were waiting.

"Can we get you anything?"

"No, I'll be fine. Look, I'm sorry for the outburst."

She gestured to her room and wandered off.

* * *

Sam stood there for a few more seconds before knocking on Max's door. He told him to come in. Max's room was like any typical teenager's. Band posters covering the walls, a guitar in the corner of the room, sneakers beside his bed, a half-open closet full of clothes and items he didn't want the whole world seeing. He looked sheepish as Sam closed the door behind him.

"Reminds me of my room when I was a kid."

Max looked around but didn't reply. "You mind if I take a seat?" he said, gesturing to the computer desk chair.

"Free country."

Sam sat down and glanced over his desk that was full of schoolbooks. "You had one year left to go?"

"Yeah."

"What were you gonna do after that?"

He sighed. "Does it matter?"

"Not right now but you never know. The lights might come on."

"You don't believe that."

He shrugged. "Whether they do or don't, the future still matters. You matter. Especially to your mother."

Sam got up and went over to the window and closed it.

"Is that why you're here? To give me some lecture. Did my mother put you up to this? If so don't bother. I don't need to hear it."

"No. Maybe you don't." He paused. "Tell me, Max, are you having a hard time sleeping? Your mother said she was. I mean after all you two went through with those intruders."

"I sleep fine," he said slumping down on his bed and grabbing up a music magazine. He flipped through it pretending not to listen but Sam could tell he was just doing it to act like he didn't care.

"You know, the first person I killed was an accident. I still remember his face," Sam said.

That piqued his interest. His eyes peered over the magazine and met Sam's.

"Before I managed to land a job here, I was a rookie cop based in Bangor. Anyway. My partner and I got a call of a robbery in progress at a jeweler's. Two guys burst into the store with guns raised, and did a smash and grab. We cornered them about four blocks from the jewelry store. It was nighttime. We had no details other than they were masked, and wearing black. So... my partner swerved the cruiser down this alley. He jumped out and took off after one while I went for the other one who scaled up a fire escape. Eight stories high. I ended up in a foot pursuit across multiple buildings until I cornered him on this one roof. He pulled what I thought was a gun. I took the shot. When I reached him he was bleeding out. I pulled the mask off and it was just a kid. No older than fourteen." Sam shook his head. "I still see his face to this day."

"You lose sleep over it?" Max asked.

"I did. For many months. I drank a lot. I snapped at

people. I questioned whether or not I wanted to be a cop." He ran a hand around the back of his neck.

"So what changed it for you?"

"Time. Time changed it. That and having someone to talk to about it. I sat with a therapist and eventually I stopped having nightmares."

"What's that got to do with me?"

"I'm just saying that I get the need to act out, but your mother cares for you. You're all she's got. Just give her a heads-up in the future. Let her know where you're going. You want her to treat you like an adult. Treat her like one. And if you need someone to talk to, I'm here."

Max nodded.

"Anyway, where did you go?" Sam asked.

"Just fishing."

"Catch anything good?"

He screwed up his nose and shook his head. "No. Nothing."

"Well speaking of fishing. I need to speak with the community. They're not gonna like it," he muttered as he got up and headed for the door.

"Why?"

"Well. I shouldn't be saying this as it hasn't happened yet but we got a visit from FEMA officials today, and the military. They want all coastal towns to be involved in contributing to the cause."

"The cause?"

"The camps," he replied.

Max pulled a face. "Why don't they just come and do it themselves?"

"Many hands make light work," Sam replied. "They want to focus on the camps, not on bringing in supplies. They want us to do that."

"Are you…?"

"I don't think we have much choice."

Max snorted. "Why don't you tell them to do it?"

"I did. They didn't listen."

"Perhaps that's why Ray fought back," Max said quietly, thinking Sam didn't hear.

Sam screwed up his face. "Ray? Who's Ray?"

Max got this look on his face as if he realized he shouldn't have said anything.

"Max. Who's Ray?"

He groaned. "He heads up the Maine Militia."

"The militia?" He stared back at him. "How do you know them?"

"I... Look, don't tell my mother. She'll just freak. Besides, I'll be eighteen in a month and—"

Sam walked back to him. "Max."

He grimaced. "That's where I was today. I mean, I didn't go out to meet them, so to speak. Our paths crossed, you could say."

"They're in Castine?"

"No, on an island. Not far from here. They're from Belfast across the bay but had to leave because of a run-in with the military. They were taking everything that the townsfolk were bringing in."

"The militia was?"

"No. The military. FEMA."

"Everything?"

Max nodded.

"But they told us they only wanted a portion."

"Well maybe they do from us, but that's not what happened in Belfast. They took guns, ammunition, fish, canned food, dry food, yeah… pretty much cleared them out. Ray and his guys stepped in and stopped them. They took it back and well…" he trailed off.

Sam went over to the window and looked out. He could see a few small lights in the distance. Fires? Maybe lights powered by solar generators? "So they're hiding out on an island?"

"I wouldn't call it hiding. Staying low until the military raise their head again."

Sam nodded. "How many are there?"

"Uh, twenty, maybe thirty."

Sam pondered it for a moment. While he didn't know how things would play out in Castine, he was interested to find out what Ray knew about FEMA. Up until that point the only information they got came from Teresa and she was the least reliable source of truth. "You think you could take me to see them?"

Max's brow furrowed. "I guess."

Chapter 9

Death could strike at any moment. They could feel Billy's eyes boring into the back of them as they hiked by day, and camped at night.

Four days.

Four days of grueling hiking.

Four days since Billy had vanished.

In that time they'd put in nearly twenty miles a day, passing through the state of New York and gunning for Kent, Connecticut. They kept it simple. Using streams and rivers as a water source, hunting rabbits and using what little supplies they had left to get them through each day. They avoided Warwick and Chester, but had to pass through Newburgh to cross the Hudson River. They'd argued a little but it was mostly regarding Billy.

Landon knew he was following closely, just waiting for his opportunity. So why hadn't he taken it? There had been plenty of opportunities. This led Beth to believe he was gone but he didn't buy it. Even though they hadn't seen or heard him, he was out there. The indication that he was near was Grizzly frequently turning his head and growling. Beth said it was probably a cougar but Landon didn't think so. Still, each time they looked into the forest, no one was visible. While Billy didn't have a rifle or handgun in his possession when he left the camp, he still posed a threat. Branches could be sharpened and rocks could be turned into weapons. It wasn't a matter of if he would strike, only when.

Landon wanted to send Grizzly out to hunt him down but Beth was against the idea. "I'm not sending my dog after that maniac," she'd said.

"He doesn't have a weapon, Beth. You should have let me go after him. At least that way we could both sleep at the same time."

"My father warned me about this. I don't think I'll ever let my guard down again. "

"You didn't let your guard down," Landon said. "We trusted him, just like we did Tim and Nancy."

"Yeah and where did that get us? It took us almost a week to replenish our gear, and we still don't have half of it. Now we're looking over our shoulder every two minutes and I have to have Grizzly on a leash, otherwise he'll take off into the forest."

They had been rotating shifts at night.

Nights were always the hardest.

All it would have taken was a rock thrown at him or to have Billy creep up on the campsite and they could find themselves in a fight for their lives. That's where Grizzly came in handy. Even the slightest movement caused his ears to perk.

Landon sighed and reached down. His hamstrings were sore from walking but he refused to let it slow him down.

"I think we should stop in Pawling," Beth said.

"Why? It's only one more day until we reach Kent."

"Because we are down to our last few bullets, and I have no arrows and we have no food left."

"So we set a few traps."

"No."

"Look, we agreed to avoid the towns as much as we could."

"As much as we could? " she repeated. "You didn't want to stop in Warwick or Chester, and you wouldn't stop in Newburgh."

"You saw that group."

"We could have found something."

"Yeah, well, I say we keep going."

"He's not out there, Landon."

"You don't know that."

"No. I don't, but after four days you would think he would have shown himself. He had no gear, no ammo, nothing, Landon. Now for the millionth time. Listen to me. He's gone. He's either dead or he split while he had the chance." She stared at him. "It's been four days. Think about it."

He was thinking about it.

Hell, he hadn't stopped since his close brush with death.

They continued on. The trail elevation went from four hundred to seventeen hundred feet giving them gorgeous views. They passed by multiple lakes, rivers and ponds and saw homes dotted along the wooded shoreline. The Hudson River was full of boats, people out fishing, trying to catch anything to survive. At one point they found they had lost sight of some of the white blazes and had to double back along a footpath, which they came to discover wasn't the AT. Landon was sure he would see Billy when they backtracked but he wasn't there. A part of him hoped he was dead but he was starting to think that the reason Billy hadn't attacked was because he knew they were expecting it. By holding off he was lulling them into a false sense of security. Once they lowered their guard he would strike.

As they began to see signs for Pawling, New York, population 8,463, Landon felt his pulse speed up. While the trail wasn't safe, it somehow felt safer than passing through a town. What Tim and Nancy had told them had stuck with him. Five and a half months since the blackout gave society plenty of time to revert back to their animal instincts. They'd already witnessed it in Mountain City.

Old Route 55 soon merged with Main Street, and as they approached from the west they noticed its residents had followed the same path that other towns had by setting roadblocks. "Look... Beth."

"We're going through the town. We need supplies, Landon."

He lowered his head and sighed. It wasn't like he could argue but needing and getting were two very different things. There must have been thousands of people who were in need. Time would have given the townsfolk a different mindset. Long gone were the days when towns would offer help. It was every man for himself, and if it wasn't, they had to question their motives.

"It's blocked off. Let's cut through there," Beth said, pointing to a suburban neighborhood. In the days after losing their gear they'd done the same thing. Entered towns, broken into homes, rooted through abandoned buildings and gathered what they needed, but in all instances they had faced danger. Mostly it was those trying to protect the little they had left but there were a couple of towns that were under the control of military. Whether they were government or militia, that was hard to know. Those towns they'd given a wide berth. But it was to be expected. For some the blackout meant desperate times, for others opportunity.

They crouched and cut through a yard at the back of a row of two-story homes. Many of the windows were smashed, a door had been torn off and garbage was everywhere. The smell of feces and piss carried on the wind as they entered a home that looked as if it had already been looted.

Blood was smeared on the floor; the walls and one section of a sofa were saturated. Landon followed the trail of red with his gaze and could almost envision what had occurred. Someone had shot the homeowner in the back of the head from outside, then dragged the body out.

While Beth and Grizzly explored, he waited on the back porch looking at the trail that disappeared off the deck across the grass and paving stones, and stopped at a dark brown shed. Landon looked over his shoulder and saw Beth opening cupboards. Holding the only handgun that had bullets, he crossed the yard and tugged on the shed door. It was stuck. He pulled hard and as soon as it swung wide he was hit with the smell of death. His gag reflex kicked in. He held a hand over his mouth as he looked upon four decayed bodies stacked on top of each other.

Why move them unless whoever had done it had chosen to stay in the house? Landon jogged back to the home, scanning the windows. He stopped for a second and thought he saw someone in a neighbors window but when he looked again they were gone.

"Beth. Hurry it up. I have a bad feeling about this town."

"Absolutely nothing. Empty boxes. No cans. Nothing." She slammed one of the cupboards. "Let me check upstairs."

"No! Let's go. We'll try another house."

She glanced at him and could tell he was on edge. "All right."

They exited and crossed over a fence that had collapsed or been knocked down and went into the neighbor's yard. Landon kept looking over his shoulder. A shot of fear went through him as he looked up at the windows. The house beside it was in a similar state except there were no trails of blood. While Beth went through the cupboards he went upstairs and checked the bedrooms. Everything was in a state of disarray like someone had been through the home and ransacked it. There were holes in the walls, graffiti, and trash scattered everywhere. Landon made his way to the rear window and looked out. It gave him a good view of everyone's backyard. He then went to the front of the house and that's when his heart nearly stopped. The same woman he'd seen up in the window was speaking with a group farther down the street. They looked to be your typical suburbanites. The kind of people he might have seen talking among themselves on a

Saturday morning while cutting grass. Except they weren't typical now. They looked disheveled, desperate and armed. The very second the woman turned their way and pointed he knew they were fucked. The group took off, running fast towards the house.

"Beth. Beth!" he yelled, backing up and launching himself down the stairs in three strides. He slammed into the wall at the bottom and she nearly bumped into him.

"We need to go. Now."

"But I found some—"

He grabbed her by the wrist and pulled her with such force she knew not to argue. There was no time to tell her what was happening only that escape was the only option. They burst out of the back into the yard and took off through one neighbor's yard to the next heading south while the group was coming from the east.

Based on the distance between them and the house he knew they weren't going to be able to make it out of the neighborhood. "In there. Quick!" he said pulling her towards another home. They entered the rear door, his handgun raised, expecting trouble. They could already hear voices of people searching for them. All three of them bounded up the steps and without even having time to clear the rooms of the house, Landon reached up and pulled a cord to open the attic. A metal ladder slid down and he urged Beth to go up.

"Grizzly," she said.

"I'll lift him up to you. Come on. C'mon!" he said glancing towards the stairs where he was sure he heard someone enter the house. They moved fast and as soon as Landon was up, he pulled up the steps and closed the door to the attic. Cloaked in darkness they waited there in silence. Nothing. Not a single sound.

"What happened?" she asked.

"Stay quiet," he said. Grizzly moved on top of the wooden flooring; his nails were so long it sounded like rain tapping the roof. "Beth." She immediately got hold of Grizzly and tried to keep him still. Making his way over to a gable's slatted vents, Landon peered out and saw the group going from house to house.

He turned back to Beth.

"We'll stay here for now. When it gets dark we'll head out and leave."

"I'm not leaving, Landon, until we get what we came here for."

"You want to die?"

"We'll die anyway if we don't find more ammo. How many bullets have you got left?"

"Three."

"Yeah. Three," she said, "and I have none."

He was about to reply when they heard someone's voice. "You can come out. They're gone now." Beth flashed Landon a look. He shook his head no. "Listen, if I meant you any harm, I would alert them. Okay? Now I'm going to reach up and pull the attic door down. Do not shoot. You hear me?"

"Okay," Beth said. Landon pulled a face.

"Are you out of your mind?" he said through gritted teeth in a low voice.

"Not everyone is bad, Landon."

"Oh so because you encountered a couple of guys who didn't murder you, you think we should trust more strangers?"

Before he could finish, a woman's face came into view. She had dark wavy hair that fell past her shoulders. "Hello there," she said. "My name's Abigail. Abigail Spencer. And you are?"

"Don't come any closer," Landon said.

"Whoa. It's okay. I'm not armed. I'm going to raise my hands now." Slowly she lifted her hands to show them and then told them she was coming up and to not shoot. She was an attractive woman, not much older than him. She was wearing a white blouse, and dark black jeans with flats. She certainly didn't look as though she had been through months of suffering. It was a strange sight that was for sure.

"I'm Beth."

"Beth. And this is…" she gestured to the dog who strangely enough wasn't growling. Nearly everyone they'd met who had turned out to be a threat, the dog had growled at.

"Grizzly."

She smiled and looked at Landon.

"You with that group?" Landon asked.

"I'm a part of this community if that's what you mean. Regardless, you are in my home so I would ask you to lower the gun."

"Can't do that."

He got up and crossed over to where she was but kept his distance. He just wanted to check that there wasn't anyone downstairs. "I live alone. And they won't come here."

"Why?"

"I'll explain but again, you need to put the gun down."

Beth gave a nod. Landon was still reluctant. He lowered it to his leg but didn't put it away. "How about we all go downstairs? You both look famished."

"You have food?" Beth asked.

"I hope so. The last time I looked it was there this morning."

Although Landon wasn't comfortable, it only made sense to head down. If it was a trap, he was prepared to fight his way out.

Chapter 10

Sam thought Mick Bennington was up to his old tricks again when he got the call over the radio. "Sam, this is Jake, you copy, over?"

He rolled over in his bed and reached for his radio. Sam glanced at his clock. Six thirty in the damn morning. He'd only had five and a half hours sleep as he'd got in late from Sara's and was hoping to sleep in. What on earth was so urgent that he would contact him at this hour? He took a second to wipe sleep dust from the corners of his eyes before replying, "Copy, Jake. Go ahead."

"We got a problem down at the docks. Bennington and ten of his pals showed up here in full military fatigues, barking orders and having fishermen put a good portion of their catch in the back of a Humvee."

It took Sam a second or two for what he said to sink in.

"You want to run that by me again?"

"Just get down to the docks and fast. This is getting out of hand."

"Jake. Jake!" Sam said but he got no reply. He crossed the room and went into the bathroom to relieve himself in the toilet before taking a large bucket of rainwater and flushing it away. He hurried into the bedroom and slipped into his police uniform. One sniff of it and he nearly threw up. It badly needed to be washed but he just hadn't got around to it. He put on his duty belt, and nearly tripped as he hurried out the door then realized his boots weren't on. Sam yelled loudly into the air, frustration getting the better of him. He hated early mornings and nothing pissed him off more than waking to hear that Mick was causing trouble. He could only imagine what he was up to as he collected his boots and hurried to a horse tied up in his backyard. After losing their vehicle to a vandal, he and Carl had opted to use horses courtesy of Arlo Sterling. It wasn't the fastest transportation but it did the job.

He stroked the black mane and climbed into the saddle. The horse snorted as he set off towards the town dock. It was a good ten-minute ride from his home which was located at the end of Turner Point Road. It was a solitary waterfront property that he'd nabbed up at a bargain price after the home went into foreclosure. Sam breathed in the crisp morning air and relished the last few minutes of silence. He was getting tired of locking horns with Mick but even if he could arrest him, they no longer had room at the jail in Ellsworth.

Sam looked out across Castine, wondering what would become of the town if the military decided to move ahead and bring into effect FEMA's plan. Everything they'd worked so hard to achieve would fall by the wayside. The only reason it had worked so far was because it was fair. The moment they were required to give up a portion of their catches to the government, things would change.

Maybe Carl was right. Perhaps the best thing to do was to hang up the uniform, crack open a beer and take to the water to spend his days fishing. As it stood their hands were tied on what they could or couldn't do. They were at the mercy of the town. A recent visit to Ellsworth had confirmed the worst. There was less staff to oversee the jail and the conditions were bleak.

Now that they were five and a half months into the event and no one was offering to help local law enforcement, Sheriff Wilson had called a meeting to discuss the situation with the remaining officers and let them know that he would fully understand if anyone chose to stop assisting the community they were assigned to. A few handed over their badges and walked out, leaving only five willing to continue. Sam knew that would decrease even more over the following months now that Wilson was telling them that they couldn't send any more people to the jail as there was no room.

As Main Street curved down to the dock, he took in the sight of a crowd gathered around a large Humvee that was positioned nearby with multiple people in army fatigues. He recognized them as Mick's guys. "Shit. What is he up to now?"

At first he thought that perhaps the military had rolled into town to move ahead with their plan of forcing fishermen to give up a portion of their catch and that Mick's men had turned up to confront them. It couldn't have been further from the truth. Sam gave the horse a nudge and rode right into the midst of the commotion.

"What the deal?" he asked as he dismounted and Jake elbowed his way through the crowd.

"I think you should hear it from Mick."

They made their way through to the rear of the Humvee just in time to see Mick lash out at Pete Barnes, one of the most active fishermen in Castine. His company had been the backbone of the community for the longest time. "Hey!" Sam yelled hurrying over to get between them. "You want to tell me what is going on?"

"Ah, Deputy Danielson," Mick said in his usual smug tone. "I'm glad you can join the party. You're just in time for the best part. We're here to collect for FEMA."

"What?"

"You heard me," he said, gesturing to a few of his men

as they carried a large cooler over to the Humvee. Sam reached out and lifted the top to see the contents. It was full of fish encased in ice.

"He's stealing from us," Pete said.

"Under the authority of the United States government all catches of fish will be subject to a 50 percent contribution."

"You can't do that."

"Oh but I can."

"No I mean, who gave you the authority?"

"The town manager. I would have thought you were privy to that." He paused and smiled. "Oh that's right, you can't be trusted now."

"What?"

"Step out of the way, deputy, you are slowing the progress of my men." He turned towards the crowd and got up on the Humvee. "Just as you paid tax to the government. This is a form of tax. You are no longer able to contribute from wages, but consider what you catch your wages. We are just here to collect on behalf of

FEMA."

Sam was dumbstruck.

"He can't do that, can he?" Jake asked.

"Not while I'm overseeing this town," Sam said climbing up onto the Humvee and drawing his service weapon. No sooner had he taken it out than all of Mick's guys raised their rifles at him.

"Oh deputy, I would be very careful what you do next."

Sam stabbed his finger at him. "You are not in charge."

Mick was as cool as a cucumber. He smiled back. "You'll find we are. Speak to Teresa. In the meantime I would advise you to holster your weapon. I can't be held accountable for what these men will do if you don't. We have our orders."

Sam could smell the whiskey on his breath.

Jake had his rifle at the ready, as did three of the people they'd deputized over the past week, but he wasn't looking to get into a gunfight in the middle of a public place. There were too many innocents and Mick was crazy enough to let bullets fly.

He jumped down from the Humvee and Mick's guys went back to collecting. It was a heartbreaking sight. Not everyone had caught the same amount and yet 50 percent was taken even from the little they had. At least taxes had a system, a means of determining how much each person had to give, this was just abuse. While he understood the need for the country to work together, there were ways of going about it. He figured the military themselves would show up, not use locals to do their dirty work. There was meant to be some back and forth over the next few weeks on how to roll out the plan in a way that didn't get the community's back up. Teresa had lied.

As Sam squeezed through the crowd, those around him asked him if they could do this and all he could do was reassure them that he would look into getting this resolved as quickly as possible, and for now let them take it.

* * *

It was another hour before Teresa showed up at Emerson Hall. Sam had been waiting outside because the doors were locked. Of course her vehicle was still working but was she willing to let them use it, nope. "Deputy Daniels. Just the man I need to see."

He rose from his seated position on the steps. "Why did you lie to me?"

"Lie?" she said. She took a bag out of her trunk and juggled it while she reached into her handbag for a set of keys.

"You said that you would be alerting me to when FEMA planned on implementing their plan and then I find out today that Mick Bennington has been placed in charge."

"That's right," she said twisting the key in the lock and strolling in. He followed in her shadow. "The decision was made late last night by Harris."

She led him into her office and dropped her bag beside her desk and took a seat. He remained standing. "Whatever happened to let's roll this plan out slowly?

Whatever happened to let me speak to the community first? You know we nearly had a riot on our hands."

"I'm sorry about that but FEMA has needs right now and as a coastal town we have a responsibility to contribute to the effort."

"Oh spare me the bullshit. There are ways of doing this. You don't just agree to one thing then charge ahead the next day doing something else without making that known. I had people asking me if he could do this. When I tried to stop him his guys raised their rifles at me. Now what kind of message does that send this town?"

She lowered her head and breathed in deeply. "Like I said. A decision was made and our job is not to question why."

"Really? Tell me something, Teresa. Would you be pissed if people who earned more money than you were taxed at the same rate you were?"

"What are you getting at, deputy?"

"Pete Barnes might be able to handle a 50 percent cut on his catch as he hauls in huge loads of fish but small-time fishermen should not be gouged at the same rate. There needs to be order to this. That's why you can't just charge in there like a bull in a china shop and expect them to hand over what they have caught."

"Lower your voice, deputy," she said removing her glasses. "You think I don't know that? You think I didn't bring up that point with Harris? This town is no longer under the authority of the county, the U.S. government is overseeing all decisions. I have to go through Harris from now on. How do you think that makes me feel?"

He snorted. "Please. Next you're going to tell me that you're suffering. And yet we all know about that nice big cache of supplies in your home. Yeah. Jake told me. Now that gets me wondering. Where have you been getting that? The stores don't have any. The emergency supplies that the town had are gone." He paused. "It makes me think that you have been in bed with FEMA for far longer than what you have let on."

"Deputy."

"Don't!" he said. "I know how this works. I know this

is nothing but a power move. You knew full well that placing Mick Bennington in charge would piss me off."

"I didn't place him in charge. Stop your accusations. Harris did."

Sam shook his head. "As if he knew him. Bullshit. Harris would have asked you who besides me did you think was capable of handling the collections. I am the deputy of this—"

"Not anymore you're not," she said cutting him off and standing to her feet. "After that little fiasco in front of the colonel, I was given the unfortunate job of informing you that your services will no longer be needed. That also goes for Carl."

His jaw dropped.

"And before you say I can't do that. It's already done. Harris has spoken with Wilson. You are relieved of your duties."

He scoffed. "How are you going to protect this town?"

"Oh you thought Mick and his group were only going to be handling collections? That Humvee out there is for use in this town. The baton has been passed to Mick."

"You are joking. No. I want to hear this from Harris."

"He won't be here for another week. At which time he will assess the situation and make adjustments as necessary."

"Teresa. This is madness. You saw what Mick nearly did to that man. He would have—"

"A man who was at fault, deputy. It's already been proven."

"What, by DNA? Or by the court of Mick?"

"By the testimony of the young girl who was raped."

He scoffed. "So that's the new form of justice, is it? Whatever happened to innocent until proven guilty?"

"We are living in very different times."

"You're right about that. You are making a mistake, Teresa. Mick will be the downfall of this town. Taking orders from that asshole will cripple this community. But I guess that doesn't matter as long as your needs are met."

She scowled. "As much as I don't like Mick's approach, he is good at following orders and right now that's all FEMA wants. They don't want troublemakers and—"

"They think I'm a troublemaker."

"I wasn't going to say that but…"

He shook his head and placed his hand on his duty belt.

"I was told to collect your badge and firearm," she said. "Leave them on the desk here before you leave."

Sam took out his badge and tossed it down. "You can have that but tell Harris, if he wants this, come and get it!"

Teresa pursed her lips.

Sam turned to leave. He made it to the door but when he opened it, he came face to face with four of Mick's guys. "I told Harris you would say that, so he took the liberty of giving Mick some additional instructions."

"You bitch."

"Hey, don't shoot the messenger."

Sam gritted his teeth as he handed over the weapon to Holden Whitefield, a close friend of Mick's, a man with a tainted track record of his own. He cast a glance over his shoulder one final time at Teresa and then shouldered his way through the four men.

Chapter 11

Landon finished the plate of bacon, beans and eggs in record time. He hadn't tasted food this good in months. Abigail sat across from them, nursing a cup of coffee. She had this smile on her face as he wiped bean sauce with fresh buttered toast. "You were hungry. There is more where that came from if you'd like some more."

He washed down the last bite with a glass of orange juice, still keeping his handgun leveled at her under the table. Abigail asked if she could give Grizzly a few rashers of bacon, and Beth nodded. She tossed three pieces to the dog and he swallowed them without even chewing.

"How do you still have food after five and a half months?" Landon asked.

"This is a tight-knit community. It also wasn't the first time we'd had a blackout. We learned our lesson a long time ago that if you fail to prepare you suffer. Several of the town council members are ex-military. They came up with a program similar to the ones you see at Christmas."

"Program?" Landon asked.

"C'mon, you must have seen them. Many of the large chain grocery stores around Christmas give shoppers a way to donate to those in need by buying a few extra cans or purchasing a bag of groceries. It's a one-time event that usually does well. Anyway, we decided to do something like that on a smaller scale; an ongoing way for the community to donate a can here, a can there toward our town's emergency program. We've had that running for over three years." She took a sip of her coffee. "So, you can imagine how much canned and dry food we accumulated in that time. Sure, a good portion of it has passed its expiration date but it's food nonetheless."

"So the community donated this?"

"Yeah, think of it like when you go through the checkout at the grocery store. Quite often they will ask you, do you wish to donate two dollars to the Diabetes Foundation — or whatever charity. Most people do it. It's not much to ask and most agree. Look, it wasn't mandatory and the town council sent out flyers to every home to let them know in advance that we were rolling out the program. It wasn't exactly foreign. People were already trained to donate, if you can call it that."

"That's pretty smart."

She leaned back in her seat. "Well it's not rocket science and it's easy to implement. The only hurdle is getting people to donate but so many of the people in our community were either directly affected by the blackouts, or knew someone close who was, that it only made sense to have something in place that would benefit the community."

Right then the back door opened and an unshaven man with a rifle slung over his shoulder poked his head in. "You good?"

"We're doing fine, Ryan. Thank you."

Unbeknownst to them, while she was outside cooking up food on a charcoal grill, she'd invited a few of the people who were searching for them to come inside and meet them. At first, Landon thought it was an ambush and rose to his feet ready to squeeze off a few rounds. Fortunately Abigail was quick to reassure him that they were safe and she'd only done so to allow them to return to their posts.

Ryan ducked back out and Landon turned back to her. "What's the deal in this town?"

"With what?"

"We've traveled through a number of communities and this is the first we've come across where you seem to actually be working together."

"Well that's unfortunate. Though I imagine there are towns across the states like us. We don't consider ourselves any better. We were just a little more prepared than maybe others were."

"And yet you still have this large cache of food after all these months. I would have thought by now discord, jealousy, greed would have at least got the better of the people in this town."

She nodded and took another sip. Her relaxed demeanor seemed out of place in a country that had been torn apart by violence at the hands of desperate people. "I didn't say we didn't have problems, Landon. Four doors down from here an entire family was murdered for what they had."

"The bodies in the shed?"

She nodded.

"Why haven't you buried them?"

"Because they are there as a warning to any others."

He frowned. "What? I don't understand. Are you saying these people were the result of a home invasion, and you didn't bury them?"

"I think you have misunderstood. That family weren't the victims. They were the perpetrators." She paused and studied him as if gauging his reaction as he processed what she was saying.

"You're telling me the community killed them?"

"The community dealt with the situation."

"You couldn't have just exiled them from town?"

"And risk having them return? They killed, covered it up and lied because of greed."

"But killing, how does that make you any better than them?"

She smiled and glanced at Beth who was listening intently. "Do you believe in capital punishment, Landon?"

"I think it has its place in a society with a fair justice system."

"Then this is no different."

There was a long pause as he contemplated it. "But in all those cases, those punished are judged, and go through the justice system."

"That system doesn't exist. And, even when it did, there were those who got away with murder. The fact is, that system was created by people determining what was right based on rules, regulations, human rights and so on. I'm afraid in this new world, Landon, we don't have the luxury or even the time for that. Jailing people is a thing of the past. From what you've told me of your journey, you know yourselves... split second decisions must be made for people to survive." She rose from the table with her cup in hand, went over to the sink, placed it in a bowl of soapy water and began washing it. "No one in this town goes without. No one has more than anyone else and that includes people like myself who oversee decisions."

"Are you the mayor?"

"No."

"Chief of police?"

She chuckled. "Far from it."

"Then why do you get to decide?"

"I don't..." she said, turning. "All decisions go through a group of twelve council members. These are people that have already proven themselves in the community. People that residents trust." She took a deep breath. "In the five and a half months since the blackout only two families have been murdered in Pawling. The one that was stolen from, and the one that stole. And that was within the second month. Since then we have operated with zero murders. If that is not a testimony, I don't know what is. The workload is shared. Food is equally shared. No one goes without. So far it's worked."

"And yet we breached your town. Surely others have too. So what's the point of a blockade?"

"You didn't breach. We allowed you in."

Landon looked at Beth, then his gaze slowly shifted back to Abigail. He tightened his grip on the gun beneath the table. She smiled as if knowing what he was thinking. "Don't worry, Landon, it's not like that. Could we have walled off the town by now? Perhaps but the labor, the time would have been extensive and for what? What message would that send to roving gangs? Walls are built to protect. Protect what? We might as well have raised a sign saying... we have food... come and get it." She snorted. "No. We aimed to portray our town like any other town in the area. The blockades on the roads are there to stop vehicles. It's pretty basic security. The population here, minus those who left, is just over one thousand. We work together. There are shifts that rotate every four hours, and everyone gets two days off a week. So... along with a cache of food built up over the past three years we have more than enough incentive for people to continue to work together. No one is forcing a gun to anyone's head. No one refuses to help."

"And yet we got in."

She smiled. "I told you. If we refused you entry, how will others learn?"

It was a lot for Landon to take in. Since North Carolina they had yet to pass through a town that wasn't empty, destroyed or under the rule of violent, scared and desperate people. There was no time to fathom how a town like this could operate and yet it wasn't outside the realm of common sense. Some towns would fare better than others if they had strong leadership.

"That's all well and good," Landon said. "But you had a cache of food for these people. Most of the towns we have ventured into didn't. They were unprepared. There was no council who had set aside food for a rainy day. My question to you is, what happens when the food runs out?"

"It won't."

Landon leaned back in his seat, finding it all a little too amusing. "Go ahead. I'd like to hear this."

"How are other towns surviving if they don't have food?"

"They hunt."

"Exactly. The only advantage we have right now is our community hasn't suffered hunger yet. We aren't just sitting back on our laurels and eating our way through this cache of food. We know eventually it will run out so in the meantime we have crews that go out and hunt in the surrounding woodland, and fish in the lakes. Meat is brought back, and preserved. Most of it turned into jerky. The fish is cooked. So, in answer to your question. When the initial cache of food runs out, we will have more than enough to continue. And by then our community will have got used to hunting and gathering. That is if the lights stay off. For all we know they may come back on." Before he could laugh at that she added, "And yet I know that may be asking too much. But I've always considered myself optimistic."

Landon shook his head. "Five and a half months and you haven't had people try to attack this community?"

"Look at our location, Landon. We are in the middle of nowhere. Visitors are few and far between. Most of the trouble we have encountered has been stopped at the checkpoints. We have enough people in town to handle an attack, and more than enough roaming the streets to spot strangers… like yourself." She finished washing her dish and placed it on the counter. "Now things could have gone another way had you not walked into my house."

"I guess we're lucky then."

"You could say that. Come, when you are done, I'll give you a tour of the town. Perhaps it will give you ideas for Castine when you return." She headed over to the door and picked up a blue jean jacket off a hook and shrugged into it.

"You said you live alone," he said making a gesture to her wedding band.

She lifted her hand. "Oh, this. Right. Yes. My

husband was away on business when the blackout happened. He never returned."

She opened the front door and beckoned them out.

Grizzly bounded out, wagging his tail.

"Don't get used to it," Beth told him. He jumped up at her and she ruffled his hair.

As they ventured out into the bright sunshine, Landon took in the sight of groups with rifles slung over their shoulders patrolling the neighborhood.

"That must have been hard on you," he said.

"Yes and no. Yes, because I care for him but no because we were in the early stage of getting divorced."

"Sorry to hear that," Landon said.

"Ah. It's fine. It wasn't infidelity. We just became two very different people. That's the only good thing that came out of this blackout. No more lawyer meetings," she said, chuckling. She waved to a group and they returned the gesture.

Landon gave a nod towards them. "How many groups patrolling?"

"This neighborhood or the entire town?" Abigail walked with her hands clasped behind her back. She lifted her nose sniffing the fresh air.

"The town."

"A hundred groups spread out through the north, east, west and south. Around four hundred people but that doesn't include those at the checkpoints. They operate in groups of four and stay within close proximity to at least two other groups just in case. We also have throughout town those we call watchers. The one that saw you was a watcher. They're positioned in homes throughout the town. Their job is to observe and notify the groups patrolling."

Landon nodded. "Don't they get tired?"

"Like I said, they only do this for four hours. With over a thousand people in town helping, twenty-four hours fills up very quickly. There are those that choose to do more and so they'll take on an extra shift but it's not mandatory. We thought that sticking to four hours would prevent burnout. So far people accept it. I know that sounds strange but this community has become closer because of the blackout. When you are out there walking beside three other people, you soon bond with your neighbor."

Landon smiled. "I have to admit. What you have managed to do in such a short time is impressive."

She cocked her head and pulled a face. "I guess so. It's not like the residents were strangers to begin with. Obviously some of them were but the community has always been a tight-knit group. We made it very clear to everyone involved what would be required but also what they would receive in return. Besides the one family who decided that wasn't enough, we've fared well."

They passed by homes where children were out playing. Abigail waved to a few people. If he wasn't aware of the blackout he wouldn't have even thought that the country was going through an event. Besides a few homes that had been broken into, there weren't any signs of violence, at least on the level of what they'd seen along their travels.

"I noticed a few homes had windows smashed. Are you still getting crime?" he asked.

"We are looking into that. Like I said, this place is far from perfect but under the circumstances I think we are doing a good job."

"Seems that way." He smiled at her and she continued giving them a tour with the promise of refilling their supplies and sending them on their way with full bellies. Landon had to pinch himself a few times. It was a stark contrast to what they'd just come through, and a welcome one at that. For the first time in months he felt a spark of hope.

Chapter 12

The FEMA rep, David Harris, unfolded the map and stared at the three counties he'd been assigned: Penobscot, Waldo and Hancock. He expected to face resistance following the imposition of martial law in the United States but with the support of the military he figured they would prevail and prevent conflict.

He was wrong.

The successful attack on a convoy coming out of Belfast had marked the beginning of a new set of challenges. They would need to rethink, adapt and tackle this threat fast before the militia group incited a rebellion. Control had been at the forefront of his mind when he was given his orders five and a half months ago. FEMA had tried to train them for such an event but no amount of training could prepare anyone for this.

Numerous camps had been set up throughout the country. His team operated out of one erected south of

Bangor, north of Bucksport and to the east of Brewer Lake in a huge space of farmland referred to as Perkins Orchard. The location was pivotal to ensure a steady flow of water and easy access to all three counties. The camp itself was the size of three city blocks with row upon row of tents, and several larger ones for the military and FEMA officials.

Contrary to conspiracy theories, they were not looking to imprison U.S. citizens or create labor camps. To do so would have been a major undertaking and would have led to an uprising, and with more civilians than military, establishing order would have been near impossible. However, since martial law had been declared he couldn't help but see them heading down that slippery slope. Actions by militia would give them few options. He was well aware that word had begun to spread that the military was going to disarm Americans, conduct warrantless searches, detain combatants, invade and assert sovereignty, block off cities and turn them into a giant concentration camp, hold Americans inside, confiscate property, food and essentials and prevent citizens from free speech, peaceable assemblies and petitioning against the government for grievances. But those were not his orders. His orders had been clear from the get-go, they were to provide emergency support and assistance to all U.S. residents in the form of food, water, medication, clothing, shelter, security and public safety.

The trouble was their ability to meet the people's needs was reliant on compliance by communities in key areas. For him that meant working closely with coastal towns and the military to ensure a steady flow of supplies to those inside the camp.

That task was easier said than done.

Not everyone was on board with helping.

That's why he'd personally gone to each and every town along the coast of the three counties to speak with town managers and discuss people contributing to the effort.

Was it a lot to ask?

By the reactions of the people, obviously.

Of course he'd considered sending some of his own people to fish at these designated communities but that would have drastically affected the camp's ability to stay on top of the influx and needs of those here. They didn't have the resources for that, all of which led them to try an agreement with town councils. Some had taken them up on it and were glad to help, others not so. Belfast had been one of the first to turn their nose up at their request. They could have let it slide but if they did that with one town, others would have followed suit. No. They had no other choice than to send in the military and enforce martial law. He'd given them fair warning. More than enough time to think over the offer. And he was fair. The initial agreement was for 50 percent of fish the community caught, but after they outright refused, he'd given the military the go-ahead to disarm citizens to avoid bloodshed.

It should have worked.

It hadn't.

The last he'd heard from Colonel Lukeman was that a

team of his men had been ambushed and all the supplies including weapons had been taken back. Harris got up and poured himself a coffee from a thermos and took a seat at his desk. The tent he was staying in was basic. One section of the tent had military cots for sleeping and the other side held desks. Everything was being done by hand. Reports. Map work. Schedules. Tasks. They had several large A-frame boards with paperwork attached, photos of combatants and a list of to-dos. The flooring was 18-ounce vinyl-coated nylon that hooked to a rope inside the walls to provide an elevated perimeter so water didn't enter. It was far from luxurious but it was lightweight, durable and extremely easy to assemble. Surrounding the camp itself was chain-link fencing.

"Mr. Harris."

David looked up from his desk. Lukeman was standing in the doorway of the tent.

"Come in, colonel." He leaned back in his chair. "What's the update?" he asked.

Colonel Lukeman was every bit a soldier. Six foot two,

granite jaw, buzzed blond hair, and wearing army fatigues, he carried himself with a confidence that only came from being in the trenches of war. "No one will say anything. The community of Belfast denies receiving their supplies back, however, our informant was adamant that's what occurred. Militia told them to bury their weapons and refuse to fish."

"They won't fish?"

"Our informant reported they are fishing farther south."

"So, you have sent men to collect?"

"Well that's the thing. Now they're fighting back."

"What?" he stammered.

"We've lost two of our men. We sent a group of ten in and only eight returned alive. They came under heavy gunfire."

"From militia?"

"No. From the people."

Harris looked down at his desk. "This is not good. Not good at all. We need to get on top of this and fast.

They're inspiring the people. If we don't put a stop to it other towns will follow."

"And yet if we kill Americans, we are liable to start a war."

"We are already at war, colonel. A war for survival." He got up from his seat and walked over to the A-frame board and thumbed through some of the paperwork. "The government knew this would happen. The director of FEMA knew this would happen. I knew this would happen."

"What do you want to do?"

"What we have done in Castine. Have the Belfast informant gather together a large group they trust to enforce martial law. Let them do the dirty work."

"Belfast is six times the population of Castine."

"And? Do you wish for your men to die? Right now they see us as a threat and they are more than willing to kill us in order to keep what they have. But will they kill their own? That raises a moral and ethical dilemma."

"That's risky."

"No more than putting your guys in the line of fire. Our job is to keep this camp afloat. If we stand back and do nothing, tomorrow one town will become two, then three and before we know it, all the coastal communities will refuse to assist."

"Why not just send in one of our group to fish?"

"Really, colonel? You want to send in the military to fish?"

"I didn't say the military. I said the people that are here in the camp," he said in an abrasive tone. "Is it really our responsibility to care for all their needs? Perhaps this way we can avoid bloodshed."

"Maybe. Maybe you're right. However, think about how that will look. You heard what that deputy said in Castine. They already think we are creating a forced labor camp. Do you really want to give them reason to oppose us? Because that's all we need right now."

"Oppose? We are helping."

"I know that. You know that. But there are those out there who have lost confidence in the government. And with the rollout of martial law, it won't be long before more groups like Maine Militia incite riots." He shook his head and paced. It was a two-edged sword. On one hand they could force the people in the camp to fish, on the other, force people in coastal towns to fish. Either way they still came out looking like the bad guy. He just had to determine what would result in less casualties for his crew.

"Maybe we are approaching this the wrong way. Perhaps we should just ask for volunteers," the colonel said. "I'm sure there are those who want to feel useful. Once the word gets out to towns, they—"

"Volunteers?" he said cutting him off. "No, the moment you ask for volunteers is the moment they realize we are operating at a disadvantage."

"Harris. They already know that."

"Somewhat," Harris replied. "Right now they are in the dark about the situation. Besides, martial law is about control. It's the government's last way of preventing civilians from doing whatever the hell they want. And right now that leads to chaos," he said turning back to the colonel. "Even if we have the assistance of towns in fishing, a time will come when we need more ammunition and further supplies. Do you think people are going to just hand them over?" he said walking over to the door of the tent. "What do you see?"

The colonel stood beside him and looked out.

"People. Hundreds of them."

"No. I see hope. As long as people have hope they will listen. Take that away and you will have anarchy. For years society has equated government with stability. Of course there have always been those who have complained, suffered and rallied against rules and regulations, but at the heart of people is a desire to follow. Our job is giving them a reason to stand behind us. That means feeding them, providing medication, giving them a sense of security. All of that requires supplies and time, and we are running out of both. I want you to take a group of your men and bring back supplies from Belfast and check in on the Castine community. Speak with your informant and then keep me updated."

"And if the people of Belfast oppose?"

"You've been through war, colonel. Do your job."

* * *

Sam observed the camp through high-powered binoculars. After giving up his weapon and badge, he'd informed Carl and Jake and had them gather together a group who'd be willing to travel up to the FEMA camp to do some surveillance. There was no point them getting up in arms over decisions if they didn't know what was happening.

He watched as the colonel emerged from the tent and that asshole Harris followed him out. "What's going on?" Carl asked, badgering him for the fourth time. Sam handed off the binoculars and dropped down from one of the trees. Jake and three others were watching out for trouble.

"So?" Jake asked. "How are they treating the people?"

He shrugged. Sam didn't want to admit it but from what he could tell they weren't being mistreated. The rumors had obviously been wrong. "They have armed soldiers patrolling but that's to be expected. None of them are abusing the civilians. From what I can see Harris was telling the truth." He ran a hand over his face. That's why it didn't make sense.

When Teresa told him that Mick was taking over, he thought that a decision like that had come about through some abuse of power, but maybe it was Teresa's inability to make wise decisions or maybe Harris was using Castine as a testing ground.

"Hey Sam," Carl said. Sam looked up. "The colonel and at least twenty military guys are heading out. But before doing so they loaded a number of boxes into the Humvees. If I'm not mistaken those appear to be weapons."

"Now where would you be taking those?" Sam muttered.

"We could follow from a distance."

"We won't be able to keep up. Not on those," he said pointing to the horses. It had been a long ride out of

Castine but it beat hiking and Mick still hadn't got his guys in enough order to prevent anyone from leaving the area.

"So what do you want to do?"

He frowned. "Head back. Nothing we can do."

"Nothing? So you're just gonna let Mick take the reins?"

"What choice do we have, Jake? Carl and I were there for the community. Teresa's made her decision. Sometimes the only way people learn is by feeding them some rope and letting them hang themselves."

He turned and walked over to one of the horses and mounted it.

"And who suffers for that?" Jake asked.

"The town is not my responsibility. Carl was right. We're better off spending our time fishing."

Jake scoffed. "Yeah. Well as long as you are happy with handing 50 percent of it over to Mick."

"I didn't say I would bring any back in."

"You know what's gonna happen."

"What?"

"Boats will be confiscated. Anyone not seen to be helping will be cut loose."

"I'd like to see him try."

"Without weapons you don't have a leg to stand on. All we have right now is our personal weapons. The rest they took."

Carl jumped down from the tree and landed hard. He let out a wail. "Ah, damn it. I've twisted my foot. Fuck! God, I hate this Harris guy. I hate Teresa. And I hate Mick!"

Sam laughed. "What about beer?"

"I'll make an exception there," Carl said, his smile returning. He extended a hand and helped Carl onto the back of the horse.

"So that's it?" Jake asked. "We just go home?"

"What do you expect, Jake… a war?"

"I thought the reason we were coming here was…" he trailed off gritting his teeth together. Sam stared at him and turned the horse away, gave it a nudge with his foot and broke away before getting into it with him. He knew what Jake expected. He expected him to lead the group against some form of tyranny but they weren't up against that, just the bad decisions of an egotistical town manager who wanted to punish him for putting her in harm's way. Even though they had caught Ian and put an end to the murders, she still went behind his back and spoke with Sheriff Wilson to get him relieved of his duties. He'd been in to speak with Wilson on the way up to the FEMA camp. Wilson refused to get involved. He'd said that at this stage the department was barely functioning. He couldn't be babysitting them and that he should have known better. There was no commendation or pat on the back that they'd caught a killer. It was all about saving face. That's when he knew his career was over. Even if the country went back to the way it was before, he wouldn't return to his position.

Maybe Teresa had done him a favor.

"Are we really heading out on the boat?" Carl asked over his shoulder as the horse trotted steadily along the road.

"Yep."

"While I'm all for it, I never figured you as one to give up."

"Who said anything about giving up?" Sam said casting a smile over his shoulder.

Chapter 13

After spending one night in Pawling, New York, their bellies were full and their spirits high as they set out for Cornwall Bridge in Connecticut, twenty-three miles away. Abigail had been kind enough to replenish their supplies with enough food to keep them going for the next four days, and additional ammo. In fact their encounter with the small town had seemed almost like a dream after the nightmare in Mountain City. And yet it attested to the resilience of the American people. If Pawling could survive and not crumble, other towns and cities could follow suit. It wouldn't be easy but Pawling had shown it was possible. Sure, they had the unusual advantage of an emergency program that had made the transition smoother but still, people were people at the end of the day, and internal fighting, greed and outside pressure from strangers could have hurt the town.

It hadn't.

It gave him hope for Castine, and for the country as a whole.

Landon took a few seconds to brace himself against a tree to catch his breath. Although he was beginning to get used to the rhythm of hiking, his age was definitely a factor. Beth on the other hand was a spring chicken, she didn't seem to break a sweat.

"You go on, I'll just rest my legs for a minute," he said.

Beth stopped and grinned. "That's what comes from eating too much. I told you to go easy."

"The food was good though, wasn't it?"

"Yeah, I have to admit I was tempted to stay."

"Well if Castine has been wiped off the map at least we know where to return."

He smiled and sat down on a slab of rock under the shade of lime-green leaves.

Passing from one state to the next, Landon had noticed how the terrain kept changing. Connecticut could be summed up in one word — countryside. The winding trail had taken them through farmers' fields, and thick woodland running almost parallel to the Housatonic River. Through the trees he could make out a flock of geese drifting downstream. For the first time since embarking on their trip he began to see the beauty of the nature. Okay, he still wasn't in love with the creepy crawlies but he understood that he was in their world and with that came a newfound respect.

"My mother loved Connecticut. She always wanted to live here."

He nodded. "Beth, you mind me asking about your mother?"

She glanced at him and a frown formed.

"What do you want to know?"

"Curious to know what she was like. You've talked about your father but not her."

Beth snapped a thin branch and tossed a piece for Grizzly to catch. "There's not a lot to say. She was... fun, caring and there for me. I was fifteen when she passed away. You know, you grow up around parents thinking you know who they are but I'm not sure I really ever knew them. I mean, really knew them. Like I knew what they did for a living, I knew they loved nature and thought that it was important to live off the grid but…" she trailed off getting a pained expression. "I didn't know that she was tangled up in drugs or an addict but according to my father that's what she was when he met her, before I was born. He'd helped her to get off it but at some point she went back to it. Kept it from him and was very good at hiding that side of her life."

Grizzly came bounding back with the branch and dropped it at her feet.

"She overdose?"

"That's what I was told. Well, not initially. I was told that she was very sick and was at the hospital getting help but that was just my father covering up for her." She threw the stick again. "Anyway, I guess she died in the hospital."

Landon nodded. "I'm sorry you had to go through that."

"Yeah, well we don't all get happy endings, do we," she

said it as if that helped her accept it.

"Your father. How did he cope with it?"

"Through the bottle. Yeah, that's where I thought he was the night your plane crashed. He was meant to come back that evening you arrived. I was on my way down the mountain and…"

"You never told me that."

"Didn't think it mattered."

"What, that you chose to put your life in danger to help me when you could have gone into town?"

She snorted. "Trust me, it wasn't exactly like that. What remains of the Ski-Doo is proof of that."

His lip curled up.

"Anyway, enough about me. What about you? You haven't talked that much about your wife or son. What are they like?"

It seemed odd that they had spent over five and a half months together and they hadn't really talked about their families. Then again, thinking about them only brought painful memories. It was easier to concentrate on survival than it was to think about how Sara and Max were holding up. After losing Ellie, he'd struggled to find the will to keep going. Had it not been for Beth nursing him back to health, and at times force feeding him when he was laid up, he may have given up.

"Max is around your age. Actually he will turn eighteen very soon. I've been there for every birthday. This will be the first I won't." He picked at the moss on the rock below him. "Sara. Well she is a firecracker. I'm surprised she's put up with me for so long."

"Why's that?"

He tossed a piece of moss. "Work. Being away from home. It takes its toll. I mean it's not like I go out of my way to piss her off or be away from them but sometimes life gets in the way. You find yourself buried beneath debt, and working all hours just to keep your head above water."

"But doesn't she run an inn or something?"

"She does but with a big inn comes big overhead. Bills pile up, and then you have two kids to put through college. It's not long before you find yourself wondering where all the money goes at the end of a month."

"College." She snorted. "Now that's something I won't get to do." She kicked at some loose stones and then threw the branch for Grizzly again.

Landon glanced at her. "What were your plans?"

"If you were to ask my father he would have said to take over his outdoor education center. But that's not what I wanted to do."

"No?"

Beth shook her head. "No, I wanted to be a nurse like my mother."

"Well that explains a lot."

"About what?"

"The way you took care of me on that mountain. Not everyone is cut out to be a nurse. It's long hours, thankless at times, and you deal with some of the worst in society."

"How do you know?"

"A friend of mine's wife is a nurse. You could say she

wasn't as fond of the job. But hey, I think you would have made one hell of a nurse."

She chuckled.

Right then, they looked over at Grizzly. He had dropped the branch and the hair on his back was up. He looked off down the trail, in the direction they were heading, and began to growl. "What is it, boy?" Beth asked. Both of them gazed that way but couldn't see anything and the only sound came from the river.

Although Landon's immediate thought was Billy, after so many days, he was beginning to think that Beth was right and he'd taken the moment to escape and probably succumbed to the elements. Beth jumped up and snapped the leash back on Grizzly. Landon shrugged back into his backpack and they double-timed it off the path, trudging through the forest trying to find a place to drop down and observe from a distance.

They took cover behind boulders farther up a steep incline and waited. Landon kept looking around as they'd passed a rattlesnake curled up in a ball just off the trail a few miles back. After the pain he endured, he definitely didn't want another snake incident.

Down below they watched as three male hikers came into view. One was in his early forties, tall, blond, wiry, intense looking with little body fat. The second one had ginger hair, pale skin and a ruddy appearance. He had a cigarette in his mouth and was leading the way. The last one at the back looked like a pear. He had long greasy hair, tattoos on his arms and was sporting a Metallica T-shirt. Around his waist was a long piece of rope that was connected to a woman's wrists. She was in her late thirties, wavy black hair cropped short, and she was wearing stonewashed jeans, a dirty white muscle shirt and nothing on her feet. *What the hell?*

"Come on, keep up!" the fat guy said tugging on the rope and causing her to stumble. Her knees drove into the earth and she wailed in pain. "Man, if I have to tell you again, I will…" He slapped her face and grabbed her by the hair to pull her to her feet.

Landon saw red and brought up his rifle but Beth

placed her hand on the barrel and forced it down, shaking her head.

The hikers continued on their way, dragging the woman behind them. Once they were out of sight, Landon rose to his feet. "Look, I understand this country has gone belly-up and we can't help everyone without putting our lives at risk but I think you know when we should help. That was it!"

"No it wasn't," Beth said.

"Beth! I think if anyone would understand and feel compassion for that woman it would have been you."

"I think you have misunderstood," she said rising to her feet.

"What is there to misunderstand? We just let them walk away."

"Landon. Stop. I didn't say I wasn't going to help. I just said it wasn't the right time." He stared back at her. "You remember back in Neva. It's all about timing. Three of them, two of us."

"We could have shot two of them."

"And risked the woman's life? No, you stay here. Let me go and follow them."

"What?"

"Well someone has to watch Grizzly."

"We'll take him with us. You saw the way he handled the guy in the cabin, and Billy."

"Yeah and all it takes is for a bullet to—"

"How's that any different than us?"

"Man, you love to argue, don't you?" she said pitching sideways and making her way back to the trail.

"I could say the same about you," he replied following her down. "Look, I know you can handle yourself."

"Yep," she replied.

"But…"

"Again, Landon, you're making assumptions. The reason I want to go alone is there'll be less chance of being heard. I grew up and hunted in woods like this. I know how to move through the forest with as little sound as possible."

"And I can't?"

"Listen, trust me. You need to trust me."

"I do," he said. "More than you know."

"Then stay with Grizzly. I won't be long. I'm just going to see."

"See what?" She didn't answer. He clenched his jaw. "And if you don't come back?"

"Give me an hour."

"An hour?" He sighed. "Beth, c'mon!"

"Landon, trust me."

"Right." He threw his arms up and took a seat on a boulder with Grizzly who sat there whining. "Yeah, I know, boy, but she goes to the beat of her own drum."

* * *

It didn't take long for Beth to catch up with them. She heard them before she saw the fat one cursing at the woman and threatening her. Beth stepped off the trail and slipped through the thick underbrush and climbed up the steep slope to get a better view of them but at the same time keep herself out of sight. Like a cougar stalking its prey she darted from tree to tree barely making a sound.

From a young age her father had taught her how to traverse wooded areas while avoiding the crunch of leaves and branches. He'd made it a game. It was like capture the flag except there were no teams involved. He would count to fifty and have her go off into the forest. If she could grab the flag without him hearing her, she would win. Months and months of trial and error, but she eventually learned where to place her feet and how quickly to move between trees.

She could hear the guy at the front telling them they would camp for the night, and then the second guy saying it was his turn with the woman. The very thought of what they were doing made her want to be ill. She crouched behind a tree and snuck a peek as the men reached a clearing and shrugged off their backpacks. Ginger boy told the wiry one to start pitching the tent while he got a fire started, and the fat guy unattached the rope and tied it off to a tree, making sure to wrap it around the woman a few times to ensure she couldn't escape. Once done, he joined the other two about ten feet away.

Beth looked back to where she'd come from. Although she'd told Landon she'd return soon, she'd only said that to get him to agree. The truth was she worked better alone.

It was late afternoon and the sun was beginning to wane so she didn't have the luxury of complete darkness for cover, but one glance at the way the men were swigging alcohol from a bottle and she knew it was only a matter of time before they would be inebriated, their reactions would be slower and she could get in undetected.

The wiry guy started cursing as he tried to put the tent up. "Come on, man, give us a hand. I can't do this by myself."

Amateurs, she thought.

"Tripp, give him a hand," the ginger guy said as he dumped some wood and began placing stones around it to create a firepit. "I swear you idiots will be the death of me."

"No, I will," Beth said under her breath.

The idea of shooting them with her rifle or an arrow was on her mind but one mistake and all hell would break loose. This needed to be controlled. Beth removed her rifle and bow and placed them beneath some thick underbrush, she then took a piece of charcoal from her backpack and marked the tree it was below with an X.

Beth reached down and scooped up some mud and covered her face, and hands. She pulled up the hood on her camo jacket and reached for her bowie knife. Blending in with her environment as best as she could, she moved in on the camp ready to kill.

Chapter 14

It was a matter of pure survival. Sam had spent his entire career as a proactive police officer. It was what was grilled into him from the moment he stepped into the academy. Don't just respond to calls, get out there, keep your eyes open and take the bull by the horns. That's what real police work is about. He could still hear one of his instructors bellowing it in his ear as they tore them down and then built them back up again. That was why he had no intention of just wasting his time fishing out on the bay and watching life pass him by. That kind of inaction led to laziness, and becoming a victim of circumstances, and he was no victim. It would have been really easy to crack open a cold one, and spend the next few months bobbing up and down in his 50-foot catamaran listening to Carl cracking jokes but that would have soon worn thin.

However, Carl didn't take the news too well.

"You want me to do what?"

"Surveillance. Monitor what they are doing."

"But I thought we were going to kick back, drop a line and bask in the sunshine."

"Carl. When have you ever known me to do that?"

"But you bought a boat."

"And I signed up to be a police officer."

He shook his head. "That makes no sense. Besides, Teresa just gave you your walking papers. They don't want us helping anymore. They've got Mick."

"Exactly. That's the problem. Teresa has no idea who she is getting into bed with."

"What, you think she's screwing him?"

Sam slapped his own forehead. "No, Carl. Not literally. Figuratively. She thinks she's doing the community a favor but she's doing them a disservice. Allowing Harris to come in and dictate how the community lives isn't just wrong, it's unconstitutional. Threatening to take our firearms so we can't put up a fight. You can't tell me that is not wrong! I swear to God, if the lights were back up he would have never said that. But because this country has gone to shit, he's pushing his boundaries, seeing how far he can go to get what he wants, to make his life easier."

"But he said it was for the camps."

"And maybe it is. But there is a way of doing it. Just telling every town that they have to give up 50 percent of their catch is bullshit! And I refuse to have a little weasel like him come in and push the good people of this town around. But that's not all. Putting authority in the hands of a child like Mick, is foolish; likewise, giving Mick free rein to do whatever the hell he likes is a surefire recipe for disaster. No, we need to be careful here. You give them an inch, they will take a mile and we'll find ourselves at the mercy of a corrupt government."

Carl laughed. "Ah, corrupt, is it? There was a time you would have died for them."

"Hey, when I signed up I didn't sign up to die — period. I sure as hell didn't sign up to take a bullet for the government. You and I chose to do this for the people.

It's always been about the people. Teresa can take the badge, the police-issued handgun but that's where I draw the line."

They were offshore, on the east side of Castine. Sam was holding binoculars up to his eyes and watching the comings and goings of Mick's guys. "Great, and it looks like his crew has got larger. Again, another reason why you don't just give power to a man who hasn't proven himself responsible."

He lowered the binoculars. "Look, will you do it or not?"

Carl groaned. "I can think of better things to do. Besides, what are you doing in the meantime?"

"Waiting for Max to show up."

"Sara's kid?"

"Yeah, seems he has established a connection with a local militia."

"Hold on a second. Are we talking about the same person? Max? That skinny little emo kid with an attitude from the inn?"

Sam brought him up to speed on what Max had told him.

Carl sat back and stared at him. "And so you think because they've already fought back, they might be of some use."

"I think they might listen. And right now we need a few more people willing to do that. We are outnumbered and besides our own personal weapons, we really don't have a leg to stand on if Mick and his crew are ordered to gather up those who are considered combative."

"Combative, as in a thorn in his side."

"You got it."

Carl threw up a hand. "But we haven't done anything."

"Not us but give it a day or two and someone down at the dock is gonna snap. Then what? If one of Mick's guys is a little trigger happy, we now have a situation that could spiral out of hand really quick. I just want to cover our asses."

Carl nodded. "Right. I see where you're going with

this."

"So you on board?"

"When have I not been?" Carl smiled as Sam fired up the engine on the boat and took it back to the mainland. Saltwater sprayed up and a gentle breeze blew across his skin as he brought the boat around to the south side near Dyce Head where he was meant to pick up Max that evening. The sun dipped down, sinking into the water and spreading out a warm orange glow as the final light of the day faded. Carl hopped off the boat. Max still hadn't arrived. "Listen, when this is all over, you owe me a beer."

"You got it."

"And Sam. Be careful."

As Carl jogged away, Sam turned his attention to Nautilus Island across the bay. He wasn't sure if going over there and conversing with militia was a good idea, as he'd heard the news about radical militia groups attacking mosques. Did he really want to get tangled up in that?

"Hey Sam."

Sam turned to see Max making his way down the wooden steps that snaked over the shore boulders. He wasn't alone. There was some funky-looking kid with a military jacket on.

"Who's that with you?"

The kid removed his baseball cap and revealed a disheveled head of ginger hair. "Eddie Raymond, at your service," he said before putting his cap back on and blowing weed in his face. "And you would be?"

"Deputy Daniels."

"Oh shit," he said taking out the weed from his mouth.

Sam chuckled. "Don't worry, kid." He took the joint from his hand and toked on it before handing it back. He blew out the smoke and nodded. "That's some good shit."

Eddie slapped Max on the back. "I think I like this guy."

As soon as they were in, Sam brought the boat out and they made their way across the water. Eddie gave him a rundown of how he'd met Max and how Ray, the head of the Maine Militia, was considering having them join his group.

"Join the group. You two?"

"Yeah, why not? My pops was in the military," Eddie said. "Nothing to it. They give you a gun, you run around shouting in people's faces and acting all hard and shit. Anyone can do it."

Sam snorted. "Yeah, I think there's a little more to it than that." He looked at Max. "Where did you find this kid?"

"Hey, you'll see," Eddie said. "These guys know the deal."

They all went quiet as the boat bounced over small waves and made it closer to the dock. Before they had got within twenty yards, three guys in camo fatigues came down the dock, guns raised at the ready. Eddie stood up and yelled, "It's okay, boys. Just us." He turned to Sam. "They are a little eager. Don't mind them. I got this."

Sam found the kid amusing. He acted like he was already one of them.

It was clear he wasn't the moment the boat knocked against the dock and Eddie hopped off with the rope to tie it off. One of the militia grabbed him by the arm and forced him up the dock. "Hey. Hey. What the hell are you doing?"

Sam looked at Max and he didn't seem fazed by it as if he expected them to act this way. "Just be cool," he said as they climbed on the dock.

All the way up onto the island Eddie just wouldn't shut up. "You need to let me go right now, soldier. That's a direct order." They shoved him forward so he continued. "I'm telling you I won't forget this. When you are operating under me, I will remember you."

Sam shook his head in disbelief. They headed up a path toward the large home, passing by a cottage that was in use by several soldiers. The ones escorting them acknowledged them with a nod but pressed on. Sam knew of the island, even had a couple of friends who'd rented it for a weekend retreat, but he'd never had a reason to head over there. There were a lot of private islands like that in

Maine. His work kept him so busy that by the time he got home he would either veg out on the couch or head out on his boat in the summer.

They were led through a set of doors into a gorgeous living area with hardwood floors, and modern furniture. It looked like a photo straight out of a home décor magazine. Everything was in the right place. The décor was expensive and yet it had that unlived-in look to it.

Two soldiers on the far side of the room, hunched over a table with a map, were talking when they entered.

"Ray."

One of them cast a glance over his shoulder. He had an average build, shaved head, dark goatee and tattoos on his forearms. "Max and…." He raised a finger.

"Eddie. Eddie Raymond." Eddie looked pissed that he hadn't remembered him.

"That's right." He then looked at Sam. "And you are?"

Max jumped in before he could speak. "He's a friend of the family, Ray."

"Sam Daniels," Sam said extending a hand. The guy

just looked at it then studied him. "Max said you're Maine Militia. That right?"

"We might be. Who's asking?"

"He's a deputy," Eddie blurted out.

That got his attention. Ray's gaze bounced. "Max. What are you doing bringing a cop here?"

"He's cool, Ray. He's just…"

Sam thought it best to nip it in the bud and get straight to the reason he was there. "I think we share a mutual concern for what FEMA is doing in coastal towns throughout Maine. I figure I could help you, and…"

"We could help you?" Ray replied.

Sam nodded. "Something like that."

"Well. I would love to help but I'm a little busy right now. Seems the military has rolled back into Belfast and hit the shoreline farther down. I'm waiting on an update. Once I—"

"Ray," another guy behind him said trying to get his attention as voices came over a two-way radio.

Ray put up a finger. "Look, I would love to chat but…

Max, next time speak to me before you bring anyone to the island."

"Not exactly your island, though, is it?" Sam said knowing full well that he was treading in uncharted waters. Ray glared at him before taking the radio and bringing it to his lips.

"Ray, this is Donnelly, you there, over?"

"Copy, Donnelly. Go ahead. Over."

"It's a damn massacre. We barely escaped with our lives. Edgar has been hit. I'm bringing him back. Get a medic on the ready."

"Shit!" Ray said as he slammed his fist against the table. At that point one of the soldiers led them out of the house. Max took a moment to chat with the soldier before he went back inside.

"I told you this was a bad idea," Eddie said shaking his head and pulling a half-smoked joint out of his top pocket and lighting it. He blew out a cloud and wandered towards the pool area.

"We'll wait," Sam said. He watched through the

windows as Ray bellowed orders to his men. Some of them rushed out. One of them was carrying a medical bag as they hurried down to the dock. It wasn't long before Ray appeared. He glanced at Sam and looked as if he wanted to say something but opted to hurry towards the dock.

Meanwhile, Eddie had taken off his boots and was dangling his feet in the pool. "I swear to God, Max, this is screwing up my chance of getting in."

"They won't let guys like you in," Sam said, observing all the comings and goings.

"Why not? The military do. Besides I turn eighteen soon."

"Doesn't mean shit to them," Sam added looking over at him. "These guys are ex-military. If they let you into their group, you'll just be a coffee boy. Nothing more than running errands."

"Screw you, man. You don't know that."

Sam chuckled, shaking his head. "No. I don't know anything. You just keep on dreaming."

"I'm going for a walk. I'm not listening to this bullshit."

Eddie got up and slipped his feet back into his boots, tossed Sam the bird and trudged into the surrounding woods. Max stayed. "You shouldn't wind him up like that."

"It's true. That goes for you too. Stay clear of them. They might be doing something good right now but I doubt your mother or your father would want you out here."

"Ah, so you tell me that now. Now that I got you over and introduced you."

"You're only seventeen, Max."

"Then I'm only eighteen. When the fuck do adults let us make decisions on our own?"

Sam chuckled and looked off towards the house.

It was a good half an hour before they saw movement down at the dock.

"You think things are gonna get worse in Castine?" Max asked.

"I don't think they will get better, if that's what you're asking. Mick—"

Before he could finish, several soldiers hurried up carrying a guy on a stretcher. When Ray reappeared he muttered something to his guys and then walked over. "Look. I know you mean well and maybe under other conditions I would have time to listen but as it stands I'm too busy. Max. Don't come back."

"Why?"

"Because you disobeyed a direct order. You want to be a part of our group, first thing is to listen and follow orders."

"But I…"

"I've gotta go," Ray said turning and patting one of his men on the shoulder to take them back down to the dock.

"Where's your other friend?" the soldier asked.

"Somewhere on the island."

The soldier had two men go off and find Eddie while they were escorted back to the dock. Sam placed a hand on Max's shoulder but he shrugged it off.

Chapter 15

A light rain fell; the steady trickle of water dripping off leaves soaked the ground as Beth made her approach. The men seemed unfazed by the change in weather, even relishing it as a howling wind tore through the trees. Gray skies overshadowed the camp making the woods feel even more gloomy. The fat one had removed his shirt and tipped his head back to catch rain droplets on his tongue, while the wiry fella tied a rubber band around his arm and slapped his forearm to get a vein to pop out. "Come on, cuz, hit me up!" he said. Ginger boy was heating up a spoon over the fire.

"Don't be so impatient."

"I want to get fucked up and then me and long legs over there are gonna have a little fun."

"Not until I've test-driven her," fat boy said raising a bottle of bourbon above his head and letting it trickle into his gaping mouth. It made Beth want to be sick.

Although she wanted to kill all three, her main concern was getting that woman to safety. At least if she was free of her restraints, she could increase the odds of her surviving.

The weather was unforgiving.

Light rain soon turned heavy. The only upside was it was masking her approach.

Beth made her way around to the tree where the woman was tied and came up from behind it. If the undergrowth wasn't as tall and thick, she was certain one of them would have spotted her. She knew how to move quietly but she wasn't a damn ninja. There was only so much Mother Nature could hide. As she drew closer, not even the woman noticed. Crouching, Beth snuck a peek around the tree and in a low voice said, "Stay very quiet. I'm here to help." She saw the woman cast a nervous glance over her shoulder but that was the extent of movement. The rest of her body was bound by the rope which had been wound tightly around her and the tree multiple times.

From behind the tree she began cutting at the rope.

While she was doing that, the ginger guy came over with a needle and stuck it into wiry boy's arm. His head rocked back and then he slumped to one side. Ginger guy laughed. "That's him out for a bit. Hey, Luke. You want some?"

"Nah, I'm sticking with the bottle tonight. Be my guest."

She continued cutting away until she was nearly through the thick rope. Just as the rope was about to give way, fatso staggered over, his voice slurring. "You and I. Tonight, my lady. I can't wait to…" He stopped and squinted. "What the…" He yanked on the rope noticing it was loose. Beth tightened her grip on the knife waiting for him to come around. She would launch herself up and jam the knife under his jaw. "Well we can't have that." He took his bottle back to the camp and headed back but before he reached the tree, Beth heard Landon.

"Here boy. Here boy! Where'd you go?"

Oh no, she thought.

Right then Landon came jogging into the camp. "Oh hey, you haven't seen a dog, have you? It's about yea high!" he said placing his hands near his knees. Ginger was right in the middle of preparing the next hit when he laid it down and got up.

"You better get the hell out of here."

Landon raised his hands. "Hey man, I'm cool. I'm just passing through. My dog broke away from me," he said lifting the leash. Fatso took a few steps away from the tree to back up his buddy. "Look, I figured you might have seen it. Dark brown, with a light-colored belly? A German shepherd. Damn dog just keeps getting away from me."

It suddenly dawned on Beth. If Landon was here, where was Grizzly?

"Are you hard of hearing?"

Ginger guy's hand slipped around to the small of his back to take out a gun but before he could latch on to it, Landon pulled his handgun and squeezed two rounds at the guy. Both shots struck him in the chest, taking him down.

Fatso reacted fast by grabbing a hatchet from his waistband and pulling back to the side of the tree, completely unaware that Beth was right behind him. She launched upwards, landing on his back like a monkey, and drove the serrated blade into his neck. He screamed in agony and thrashed around, trying to shake her off his back, but the fight didn't last long. His legs buckled and he collapsed, bleeding out. His death was fast, unlike ginger boy who was clutching his chest and slowly succumbing to his injuries. Beth bounced off fatso and made a beeline for Landon. "What the hell do you think you're playing at?"

He ignored her and went over to ginger boy, placed his foot on his chest and fired one more round, this time into his skull putting him out of his misery. "I could say the same thing about you. One hour, you said."

"It hasn't been an hour."

"Yeah, and what part of... I'm just going to see, involved you mudding up your face and risking your life with a damn knife! Seriously, Beth. Where the hell is your gun?"

"Up on the incline."

"Not exactly much help up there, is it?" he said pulling his own knife and holding it out. "I mean I've got a knife but..." Before he could finish, the woman flew past them, snatched the knife out of Landon's hand and launched herself on top of the wiry man who was in a drug-fueled haze. In a fit of rage she stabbed him multiple times until Landon dragged her off him. "He's dead. He's dead!" he repeated, wrapping his arms around her and trying to pry loose his knife. The woman dropped the knife and staggered back. Beth's gaze darted to the tree where the restraints were loose. After she cut the rope there had only been a few thin strands holding it all in place. She'd broken through that with ease.

Covered in blood, her hands shaking, rain matting her dark hair to her face, the woman dropped to her knees and wept loudly. Her body was shaking as Beth collected a blanket from inside the erected tent and wrapped it around her. The moment she smelled the scent of the men on it, she shrugged it off. "Okay, okay. You're safe now," Beth said. She looked over at Landon. "Where's Grizzly?"

"Tied to a tree just a…"

* * *

Beth took off, glaring at him. "Beth. Would you have wanted me to bring him into this? Geesh!" Landon looked at the woman then went over and crouched down in front of her. Her chin was dropped and she was crying hard.

He placed a hand on her and she flinched. "Get off!"

"Okay. All right. Look. I'm not gonna hurt you." He took a deep breath and looked over at the dead men. "What's your name?" he asked.

At first she didn't say anything.

"I'm Landon. That was… Beth."

Again no response, she just continued to weep. She was shivering hard. He removed his jacket and offered it to her. She looked up at him. When he could tell she wouldn't protest, he slung it around her shoulders and she pulled it in tight. Landon wiped the blood from his knife in some of the underbrush before placing it into its sheath. Beth returned a few minutes later with Grizzly.

"See," Landon said.

"Yeah, and somebody could have taken him, or a bear could have mauled him."

"He's fine, Beth."

She handed him over to Landon while she went up the incline and collected her rifle and bow. When she returned, Landon was rooting through the belongings of the three men to see if there was anything they could use. There was alcohol still left, matches, a couple of handguns and knives, and a few cans of beans but that was it.

He stuffed them into his backpack.

"Where you from?" Beth asked the woman.

"Gorham, New Hampshire."

"That's a long way. You've been with them all this time?"

She nodded.

"We're heading that way," Landon said. He looked inside the tent and pulled out a sleeping bag. "We'll need to take this with us," he said. "For you."

"I don't want it," she said, tears welling up in her eyes as she looked at it with revulsion. Beth shook her head at him and he threw it back inside the tent.

"She can use mine," Beth added.

"And what are you gonna use?"

"I'll be fine," she said turning back to the woman. "What's your name?"

"Dakota Larson."

"That's a pretty name. I'm Beth."

"Yeah, he said," Dakota replied.

Beth looked at Landon who was zipping up his bag. "Well we should get out of this rain. You ready?" Beth helped Dakota to her feet and led her out of the camp and back up the trail. Landon kept his gun out, looking for threats. With everything they'd been through it still didn't get any easier. For every good person they met there were many more out there looking to take advantage and kill.

* * *

It took them an hour of hiking before they made it to Cornwall Bridge. With twenty-three miles already clocked for the day and darkness upon them, they holed up inside an abandoned eighteen-wheeler cab that had come to a standstill near the bridge close to the Housatonic River. Landon climbed into the driver's side, while Dakota curled up in the back of the cab, and Beth and Grizzly sat in the passenger seat. The cab faced away from the road so any chance of anyone driving by and seeing them inside was slim. Besides, they hadn't seen anyone since arriving in the small town. Landon rubbed his hands together to stay warm and fished into his bag for something to eat. He offered Dakota some meat that Abigail had provided but she declined. Beth didn't look interested in talking as she'd already pulled her hood up and leaned back in the seat to get some shut-eye. Grizzly was the only one showing interest. "Here you go, boy," he said tossing a piece to him. He swallowed it whole and waited for the next piece.

"Dog, I swear you have hollow legs."

Beth opened one eye and stared at him.

"Hey, look, I'm sorry but I'm not just gonna let you go off by yourself. Not after what happened with Billy."

"I never saw that coming," she replied.

"Yeah, well that doesn't change the fact. Your life matters. Okay. Just as much as mine or Grizzly's. I might not have the wilderness skills or prowess you do but I'm not useless and I'm still older than you. That gives me at least twenty years more wisdom," he said with a smile. She returned it. He looked behind them at the woman. She was already asleep. "She must be tired."

"I know I am," Beth said.

"I wish I was," Landon said. "My legs hurt like hell but I'm wide awake."

"I told you not to pop those chocolate-covered coffee beans like candy."

"I know. But they tasted so damn good. I'm gonna miss that town."

"No, you'll miss the food."

"I don't know, I could have got used to it there," he said flashing a grin and looking out the window. The cab was parked about two hundred yards away from a place called the Cornwall Package Store. It was a quaint-looking building with light gray siding and dark brown shingles. He squinted but it was hard to read the rest of the sign. He could have sworn it said Beer. Landon cracked open the door to get a better look. A gust of wind blew in and Dakota stirred, looking up from the small mattress in the back of the cab. It had obviously been used by a long-distance truck driver as there were blankets, and pictures of family on the ceiling, and several fiction books tucked between the bedding and the rear.

"What are you doing?" Beth asked.

"I'll be back in five minutes. Just going to that store."

"I guess I should go with you, or are you old enough that you don't need a chaperone?" she said. He knew she was taking a jab at him for saying he didn't want her wandering off by herself.

"Touché," he said. "Up to you."

He hopped out and she said, "Ah, take Grizzly. He probably needs to go for a pee anyway."

"Come on, boy," Landon said helping him down. Landon slammed shut the door on the cab and hurried across the street. "Beer. Wine. Spirits." He smiled. "Oh please let there be something." He'd taken the bottle of bourbon the men were drinking but taking it out of his bag only seemed to upset Dakota so he'd tossed it a few miles back. Bourbon was never really his thing. He loved a good brew though. A Guinness with a nice head on it.

As he'd come to expect, the door was wide open when he approached the store. Both windows had been smashed and shelves had been dragged outside. There were multiple pieces of broken glass all over the ground. "Well, can't take you in that way. That'll cut your paws," he said. He'd got used to speaking to the dog as if it understood him. Landon went around the rear. He noticed a few cars in the lot off to the right. The doors were open on one of them, windows smashed on the others. He could only begin to imagine the desperation people went through in those early months. He was oblivious to it all on the mountain. All he could hope for was that Sara and Max were with others, good people, locals who would help each other. Any other thought just pained him.

As they often did on the way through towns, Landon searched the vehicles for anything of use. Nothing. Everything was gone. All over the seats were paperwork. The trunk was empty too except for a tire iron. He already had a knife so he left that there. Casting a glance to the rear of the store, he crossed the lot and stopped at the door. Before he entered he banged on the door a couple of times. It had become routine. The last thing he wanted to do was spook someone who was armed. At least this way he could give them a chance to exit or let him know it was occupied.

Landon looked over his shoulder a few times before he gave the door another hard knock. When he got no answer, he took out his flashlight and shone it into the store to check for broken glass. Satisfied that no one was inside, he entered the store unaware of desperate, dirty faces watching him from the tree line.

Chapter 16

Max had made arrangements to have Eddie stay at his place for the night as he assumed they would be back late from Nautilus Island. The visit lasted no more than an hour. It was utterly pointless. He now wished he hadn't told Sam about them. Eddie strolled into his room and dived on the blowup mattress Max's mom had set up for him. He bounced slightly. "Your mom seems pretty cool."

"She has her moments," Max said tossing his bag down at the end of his bed.

"Kinda hot too."

"Dude."

"What? I'm just saying. She's got the whole MILF thing going on." Eddie turned on his side and looked at him. "So I guess that's it. The end of our adrenaline-fueled career in the militia."

"I wouldn't have exactly called it a career," he said,

kicking off his boots and laying back on his bed with his arms folded behind his head. "Man, I'm just pissed the way it went down. I shouldn't have brought him over."

"Duh! I could have told you that. Cops and militia are like oil and water. Why didn't you run it by me first?"

Max gave him an eye roll.

"Look, it's probably for the best. Though I was looking forward to the round table sessions."

"The round table?"

"Yeah, you know when one of them reads the Constitution and the rest jerk off to it." They both burst out laughing. "I've never known people to get so worked up and excited about the Constitution. Geesh. My old man was the same." He stood up and got all theatrical speaking in a deep voice. "We have the right to bear arms. No one is taking away my right. Please. Nobs." He laughed and sat down cross-legged and pulled out his bag of weed. "Ah, screw them all. Besides, you heard what Sam said, we would have probably just been their errand boys. There's one thing I'm not. I'm no fucking errand boy."

He crumbled some of his weed into a rolling paper.

"Eddie, you can't smoke that in here."

"I wasn't planning on it," he said, rolling one out and licking it. He got up and went over to the window and pushed it open. "Here, give me a boost."

When Max didn't move fast enough, Eddie groaned and dragged over one of the large computer subwoofer speakers and used that as a step to climb out the window. Max sank his feet into his boots again and followed him out.

"Man, you have one hell of a place here. Great view. If I was you I would change rooms every night." He lit the joint and took a huge hit on it before passing it to Max. Both of them sat on the roof that jutted out from his window. When he was younger, he and Ellie would climb out there in the day and lay back on towels to get a suntan. His mother would go ballistic, worried they would fall off, so they promised they wouldn't do it again. They still did. Max blew smoke out the side of his mouth and handed the joint back.

"What if we proved ourselves?" Max asked, turning to him.

Eddie squinted as smoke went in his eye. "What?"

"The only reason they would have us running errands was if they didn't think they could trust us for anything else. But what if we could prove them wrong?"

He shrugged. "And how would we do that?"

"By becoming a fly in the ointment."

Eddie gave a confused look. "Okay, look, I know this weed is some heavy shit but… what?"

"Mick Bennington. A local here in town has been put in charge of overseeing the collection of supplies. At the moment, that's 50 percent of the fish coming out of the bay. According to Sam, most folks in town are pissed and they would give anything to get that back. Now the military gifted them with a Humvee to bring it back to the FEMA camp just south of Bangor. Before I met up with Sam today, I spoke with one of his guys to get more details. Seems that load doesn't go back until the morning. You up for a joyride?"

Eddie smiled. "You're thinking of stealing it?"

"Actually I was thinking of sinking the bitch at the bottom of the bay."

Eddie grinned as he shook the joint in his face. "Kid, I like the way you think. But how?"

"Ah leave that to me."

"Max!" Sara bellowed. He leaned his head inside. "You better not be smoking weed."

He looked at Eddie who had the giggles. Max tapped his leg. "Come on, let's go." Eddie tossed what remained of the joint and they climbed back in. Max collected his backpack and shoved inside a hoodie, along with a couple of bandannas. He made sure his Walther was in the bag and then he went out into the hallway and told his mother that he was going to slip out for half an hour and see if he could go and speak with Sam about something.

"Concerning what?" Sara bellowed up.

She never got her answer as he'd already climbed out the window. Both of them made their way down to the edge of the roof and jumped off. As soon as they were on the ground, they collected their bicycles from the shed and set off for town. "You still got your piece?" Max asked.

"Never leave home without it."

"Good as we might need it."

They followed the winding road. With no streetlights the island was cloaked in darkness, the only light came from a crescent moon. "Maxy boy, tell me something. If they allow you in the militia. You gonna leave home?"

"Depends."

"On?"

"If you'll be my errand boy." He cracked up laughing and Eddie tossed him the bird. It didn't take long to make it down to the docks. They veered off Water Street and tucked their bikes behind the Maritime Academy Waterfront Campus and climbed up on the roof using a drainpipe. The roof provided a good view of the dock. Max handed Eddie a bandanna and told him to cover the bottom of his face. Eddie was already wearing a hoodie so

Max pulled his out and slipped into it. The last thing he wanted was for someone to figure out who he was. Eddie wasn't a local, so even if they saw him they wouldn't know who to contact, but him... Most in town knew him because of the inn. Max reached into his bag and brought out a pair of NV binoculars his old man had bought him several birthdays ago. Crouched over and getting close to the lip of the roof, he brought them up and scanned, adjusting the focus. Two times he'd seen the Humvee over the past day, on both occasions it had been down at the dock.

"Is it there?"

"Yep. But so are four armed guys."

"Can I take a look?" Eddie said. Max handed the binos to him and he peered through. "Well that rules that out. Let's go."

"Seriously? And you wanted to be in the militia?"

"Hey, I'm all for going for a joyride but getting shot was not on my agenda for the night. I figured we'd get baked at your place and have your hot mother cook us up a breakfast in the morning." Max jabbed him in the arm. Eddie snorted. "No, in all seriousness. How do you expect us to get by them?"

"I don't know yet but I'm sure an opportunity will open up. We just need to be patient. They can't watch over that damn thing all night."

He went back to observing while Eddie rolled himself a joint. "Is there ever a time you are not puffing the magic dragon?"

"No TV. No Internet. What the hell do you expect me to do?"

Twenty minutes passed before Max noticed two of them step away from the Humvee. "That's it. Go on. On your way." They didn't go far. Only a few feet before they stopped a kid on a bike. "And who might you be?" he said adjusting the focus. "Rodney Jennings. You sellout," Max said.

"Who?" Eddie asked.

"Ah this university guy. He's made a name for himself on the island by coming up with a way to create ice." He lowered his binoculars. "That's right. If they're not taking tomorrow's load until the morning, they need ice to keep the catch they took this morning fresh." He brought up the binoculars again. "Exchanging ice for fish. Of course."

Eddie sidled up to Max. "Let me take a look."

Max didn't hand him the binoculars as the cogs in his mind were spinning. "I think I have an idea. Come on, let's go." He led the way, heading down. They left the bikes stashed behind a dumpster and stayed close to the rear of the building, making their way over to Water Street.

Sure enough a few minutes later Rodney came pedaling around the corner, whistling to himself like all was well in the world. Max reached into his bag and pulled out the Walther P99 and tucked it into the back of his waistband. He gave Eddie a tap on the shoulder and they moved into the road to make Rodney stop. He came to a screeching halt, slamming his brakes, nearly going over the top. "What the hell?"

"We're gonna need that bicycle."

He frowned. "Max?"

Oh great. Max pulled down his bandanna. "Yeah, it's me. You want to keep it down," he said gesturing for him to head over to a narrow alleyway. He didn't want to have the conversation in the middle of the road. Eddie kept a tight grip on the bike to ensure Rodney complied.

"Does your mother know you're out here?"

"Look, Rodney. I need the bike and a load of ice."

"But I just delivered what I had."

"I know. I need more."

"Well… I guess I could make more but… Why?"

"Doesn't matter. How often are you taking ice to them?"

"Every few hours. Until the morning. They said they'd only need me to create it on certain days of the week when they bring in loads of fish. They're paying me in…"

"Fish. I know," Max said.

Rodney's brow furrowed. "Look, I don't know what you guys are up to but unless they see me bringing ice, you won't get near that Humvee. I'm guessing that's what you're after, right?"

"University students. I never liked them. Too smart for their own good," Eddie said. "Maybe I should put a cap in his ass right now," he added bringing up his Glock.

"Eddie."

Eddie reluctantly lowered his gun.

"It's not smart. It's just common sense. You're not the first who's stopped me tonight to get information about those guys."

"Oh no?" Max said frowning. "Who else did?"

He looked around a few times. "Deputy Daniels. Yeah, him and Carl came by a few hours ago. Said they were watching from one of these buildings around here."

Max smiled. "Great minds think alike," he muttered under his breath.

"What?"

"Nothing. Look, would you do something for me?"

"Not if it's gonna get me into trouble. Right now this is the only gig I have. I don't fish. Nor does my mother. I'm kinda depending on this."

Max's mind was still going. He had time to think this through but without more ice the chances of getting those guys away from that Humvee were slim to none. "Let's head back to your place. Create some more ice. Load it up and we'll go from there. How's that sound?"

"Well it doesn't sound good," Rodney said.

"Yeah? Well how does this sound?" Eddie said bringing the gun up to his head. Rodney flinched, a look of fear masking his face.

"For God's sake, Eddie. Put that down," Max said. "I just need this one thing, man. I promise you won't get in trouble."

"Why is it that I don't believe you?"

"Well do you believe this?" Eddie said, lifting the gun for the third time. Max ran a hand over his face.

"Ah screw it. Maybe you're right," Max said pulling his gun and pointing it at Rodney. He shrugged. "Can't beat 'em, join 'em," he said before gesturing for him to get his ass moving.

* * *

Forty minutes later, Sam stubbed a cigarette on the floor inside a home one block away from the docks. It was owned by Gene Andrews, a guy who ran a small tailor's on the lower floor of his home. He was one of the many locals who was against the government, and that was before the blackout. Sam had brought his uniform to him a couple of times to have him take up his pants. It should have been a two-minute drop-off. It always ended up with him listening to Gene drone on about how the government were criminals. It didn't matter who got in as president. They all sucked in his eyes. Praise them up and drag 'em down. It happens every election, he would say. No, I prefer to just give them the middle finger. Yeah, he was a fiery one.

Sam sat on a chair by the window looking down at the docks while Carl sat across from him smoking a cigarette. "C'mon Sam, what did you expect him to say? Militia go to the beat of their own drum. Now had you sent Sara over I expect the outcome would have been different."

"Why do you always have to go there?"

"I'm just saying. A pair of long legs and a cute smile do wonders. That's why women make the best spies. They are unsuspecting."

"Bond was male."

"Ah yes, but haven't you heard they're bringing in a female Bond?"

Sam glanced at him.

"I'm serious. A gorgeous black girl. Forget her name but hey, it's 2019." He chuckled.

Sam returned to looking out. "Well, looks like ice boy is back again."

"You have to admit. That's kind of smart not telling them the formula and trading for fish. Supply and demand, my friend," he muttered.

There was silence for a minute or two.

"Oh shit," Sam said.

"What?"

Sam chuckled. "Rodney just collided with a vehicle. A stalled one. What the...?" He frowned.

"He's probably drinking or getting high from the

fumes of mixing all that shit up. What's in that anyway?"

Sam didn't reply. He was leaning forward on his chair adjusting the focus on the binoculars. "Three of the soldiers have come up to help him. The ice went everywhere. They're scooping it up and—" he paused. "What the hell? Who's that?"

"Who's what?"

"Two armed guys wearing bandannas just put a gun up to the head of one of the soldiers. The one near the Humvee. The other three have no idea. What the..?"

"Let me take a look," Carl said reaching up.

Sam slapped away his hand. "Wait. Hold on. One of them jumped in the Humvee and… fired it up. Oh shit."

"Sam. What?"

"A fight has broken out between the soldier and one of them. The soldier dragged his…" His eyes widened as he saw the bandanna pulled down. "Max?"

Crack. A gunshot echoed. One of Mick's guys stumbled back and collapsed.

That was followed by more gunfire coming from the

other three as they hurried back. An engine roared to life, and the Humvee peeled out.

Chapter 17

The inside of the Cornwall Package Store was a state: bottles smashed, shelves pushed over, the till tossed into a wall, and garbage scattered everywhere. The smell of piss permeated. Landon drifted the flashlight beam over the debris. There were empty aerosol cans and bags of glue, an indication that druggies had been through there. It was a real shame that people bent on looting had gone overboard and destroyed a quaint building. If the lights ever came back on again, he had to wonder how insurance companies would handle the influx of claims and whether any of it would be covered.

Grizzly sniffed the ground and wandered while he crouched and rooted through a sea of bottles trying to find anything that was still in one piece. "I could kill for a beer," he whispered. He wasn't a heavy drinker and he never bought more than a six pack a month but there was nothing better after a hard day at work than sinking down a silky smooth Guinness while kicking back and watching the UFC or a ball game.

"Well look at that," he said picking up a bottle of wine and brushing off dust from the label. It was an empty bottle of Cabernet Sauvignon from California. It was a favorite of Sara's. A flash of memories hit him — taking her out for her thirtieth birthday at an Italian restaurant. She rarely drank more than a glass but that night they'd polished off an entire bottle. Landon could still hear her laughter in his head. God, he missed her. The way she would rake her fingers through her hair and give him lovey eyes, at least that's what he called them. He remembered her being slightly sad that she was leaving her twenties behind so he'd made a point to spoil her that night, taking her for a special meal, buying her jewelry and finishing off the evening with a walk by the harbor. She'd never been a high-maintenance woman, demanding to be pampered or expecting gifts, as long as they spent time together that's all that seemed to matter. It was the little things like opening the door on a car for her. He didn't have to do it but he saw the way her face would light up on the times he remembered. Landon lowered the bottle. He felt guilty. Since the blackout he really hadn't spent much time thinking about her. Every time she came to mind so would Ellie. He had no idea how he would tell her that she was dead and buried on a mountain in North Carolina. A twinge of pain stabbed him and he felt his eyes water. He pushed the past from his mind and sniffed as he rose and continued searching the storeroom in the back. He waded through empty boxes and empty wine bottles clattered as his boots made contact with them.

"Grizzly."

The dog hurried into the room and looked at him as if he was in trouble. He gave a jerk of the head and he followed Landon into an office. His eyes roved the room. The filing cabinet's drawers had been taken out and folders and paper covered every inch of the floor. He went around the desk and sat down in the brown leather chair and closed his eyes for a second. As he stretched out his legs his boot hit something and it rolled away. Clicking on the flashlight again he shone it under the desk and he spotted a single unopened can of Budweiser. "No. Can't be," he said, dropping down and reaching for it. Sure enough, it hadn't been opened. It was like Christmas morning. He sat back in the chair and just took in the sight of it. "Thank you, God. I always believed you existed. This is like sweet manna from heaven." He cracked it open and breathed in the sweet smell. He was just about to take a sip when Grizzly growled, and turned towards the door.

Landon didn't even need to ask him what was the matter. He lowered the can, took out his revolver and slowly got up and made his way over to the door. He could hear movement inside the store. He put a finger up to his lips and looked at Grizzly. The dog wagged his tail as if he was playing a game. Landon closed the door on the office and went over to the window and shifted it up. "Come here, boy," he said. He took a hold of Grizzly's collar and hoisted him out the window before climbing out and closing the window behind him. No sooner had he done so than he heard a shotgun cocking.

"Don't move."

"I wasn't planning on it," he replied.

"Don't look over here and drop the gun."

Reluctant to do so but convinced the guy would have shot him by now if he wanted to, he released the revolver and it clattered on the concrete.

"Kick it over here."

Grizzly growled and let out a couple of barks.

"Shut that dog up or I will."

"C'mon man, he's just a dog."

Grizzly barked again.

"You hear what I said?"

Landon stepped back and took a hold of Grizzly's collar but he wouldn't calm down. He thrashed in Landon's grip. That's when Landon saw a kid no older than fifteen pointing a shotgun at him. "Hey look, kid. You want the gun, you've got it. I don't have anything else."

"No? Where did you come from?"

"Just passing through."

"Wren, pat him down."

That's when he realized there was another person behind him.

"You do it. I'm not getting bitten by that dog," she said.

The dog barked again, this time trying to snap at the girl who was just at the peripheral of Landon's vision. He couldn't quite make out what she looked like only that she was small and sounded like a kid.

"Maybe I'll just shoot the dog."

"You do that, and I'll blow your fucking brains out," Beth said, a handgun appearing from the corner of the building outstretched at his head. Wren moved only to find herself grabbed from behind by Dakota.

"Drop it," Beth said.

The girl looked panicked. "Zeke."

"Fuck." He dropped the shotgun on the ground and Beth moved in on him, smacking him over the back of the head and causing his legs to buckle. He groaned and rubbed the back of his skull as Beth lowered and placed the gun to his head.

"Kill my dog, would you?"

"I wouldn't have done it."

"No? Sounded like you would."

"I love animals. I wouldn't. Wren, tell them."

"He's right. Please don't kill him. He's my brother. He's all I've got."

"It was just a performance. Okay?" he said raising his hands. "I had to be sure you knew I meant business."

"Yeah, well I mean business too and this is where you leave the stage and get the hell out of here," Beth replied. She rose to her feet and gave him a kick. "Go on. Go! Before I put a bullet in your head."

The kid scrambled away and Dakota released Wren. She took off after her brother and Landon rose to his feet. He looked at the two siblings as they vanished into the night. If Ellie had remained in Castine he wondered if that could have been her and Max. Everyone was in survival mode. It wasn't personal. People were desperate. Beth picked up Landon's handgun and gave it back. "You're lucky Grizzly barked. How the hell did you let them get the jump on you?"

"The same way Billy did with you," he said placing the revolver back into his holster. "I heard one of them inside the store. I managed to get out. Didn't realize there was more than one."

"One in the store? I didn't see anyone come out."

Beth took off for the rear entrance, gun at the ready.

Dakota wasn't that far behind her. Landon looked off to where the teens had gone and saw them crouched near a truck. They were still there which meant they weren't alone. Landon hurried around to the front of the store just in time to see muzzle flashes light up the inside. A volley of shots ignited. His eyes darted over to the truck where the youngsters were still waiting. Not wanting to get caught in the crossfire, Landon raced around to the rear of the store. Dakota was crouched behind the dumpster, rifle raised at the doorway. "Did Beth go in?"

She nodded.

"Shit."

More gunshots echoed.

"Beth!" Landon yelled

"I'm here."

"Pull out," he hollered.

"Easier said than done. This asshole is tearing up the floor if I attempt to step out."

Landon hurried back to the office window and peered through the glass. He shifted the window and quietly made his way in. He cast a glance at the kids one more time. The last thing he wanted was them alerting whoever was inside. He moved slowly towards the door, cracked it open and looked down the narrow corridor. Another blast of gunshots rang out on the far side of the store. Clenching his gun, he hurried towards the door that led into the main store and snuck a peek. There on the far side of the room, tucked behind the counter, was a guy reloading an AR-15. Seconds. That's all he had before he slapped that full magazine in.

Charging in, Landon launched himself at the man just as the magazine went in. Their bodies collided and the man's rifle slipped out of his hands and across the floor. Landon could have shot him but he had a feeling that this was the kids' father or guardian. Still, if it came down to it he wouldn't hesitate to end his life. On the floor he wrestled with the stranger who he could barely see as it was so dark. He slammed his face into the ground, telling him to stay still. The man refused to listen and put up one hell of a fight until Beth appeared off to his right and fired one round into his skull. The noise was so loud it almost deafened him. Landon rocked back off the dead man, his eyes widening. He looked at up Beth. "Why did you do that?"

"He shot at me."

"I had this. Damn it, Beth. I had this!"

"Oh yeah, it really looked like it. You were a second away from him grasping your handgun out of your fingers."

"Those kids out there. This was probably their father."

Beth looked back at him. "Yeah, well…" She turned around and walked off. Landon sat there looking down at the man for a minute or two before scooping up his AR-15 and fishing through his clothes for additional ammo or anything that could be of use to them. He wandered back into the office and looked out the window at the two teens. Silence gave them their answer. The girl got up and attempted to run towards the building but was soon pulled back by the older brother. She wailed as the boy tried to get her to listen to him. He looked at Landon and then led her away. Landon swallowed hard and sank into the office chair. He scooped up the beer he'd set down and drained it in one go. After, he clenched his jaw and tossed the can at the wall. What the hell were they becoming? Why did this all have to happen? It wasn't like he was afraid to kill someone but did it always have to end that way?

"Landon. You coming?" Beth's voice echoed.

And what of Beth? Eighteen and she'd already got blood on her hands. It was easy to kill, harder to deal with it after. He got up and walked out and found her collecting their belongings from the truck. "We can't stay here now," she said. "We'll keep going."

She said it in a way as if he was to blame. Maybe he was. Maybe he should have known better than to walk into a store alone. Perhaps he was meant to make decisions that survivalists would approve of, but that wasn't real. No one could determine what would happen next. He shrugged into his backpack and cradled the AR-15 as they hiked out of there and over the bridge. They continued on until they picked up the Appalachian Trail again a few miles away.

Back in the woods they hiked for several miles before Dakota couldn't go any further and they decided to camp for the night in Housatonic Meadows State Park. At least this time they were in the middle of nowhere, far from any town. They set up a tent far from the trail to avoid being spotted and made sure not to start a fire.

Landon chose to stay awake, as did Beth even though he told her to get some sleep.

Sitting on a log staring into the night, he could hear the birds of the forest, and small animals scuttling through leaves. He looked over at Beth and he could see she was just biting at the bit to speak with him. Her mouth opened and closed and then she huffed.

"You killed those men without hesitation. So why do you have a problem with what I did back there?"

He shrugged. "Maybe because I'm a father. And maybe I didn't want it to end in more bloodshed."

"You think I want that?"

"I don't know what you want, Beth."

"I want to survive."

"Don't you think that man did too?"

"I gave him a chance, he refused to listen."

"You shot him in the back of the head. He was unarmed."

She squinted at him. "What if I hadn't been around? What do you think they would have done to you? Or Grizzly?" She waited for an answer but he never gave one. "I did what I had to do, just as I did on that mountain."

"Yeah, and you haven't talked about that."

"Why do I need to?"

"Because eighteen-year-olds don't just wake up and start killing people. That shit affects the mind."

"Does it? You know how old I was when I killed a deer?"

He shrugged.

"Eight. Eight years old." She stared back at him. "I never understood at the time but later you come to realize it's what has to happen."

"That's different."

"Is it? Don't you think that animals deserve to survive? Who deserves it more? Us or them?"

Landon tossed a small twig and got up. "You're missing the point."

"Am I? Then tell me. Go on. Tell me why that man deserved to live?"

"Tell me why he deserved to die," he shot back at her.

"Because he was trying to take my life. But more importantly, he could have taken yours. And I won't let that happen."

"I'm not your father, Beth."

The words came out before he realized how they would impact her. She studied him for a second or two and got up and walked off into the forest. "Beth. Beth. I'm sorry. I didn't mean it that way. I…" Landon sighed, squeezed his eyes shut and ran a hand over his tired face.

Chapter 18

Sam burst through the rear door of the inn with Carl in his shadow. "Where is he?" he bellowed scanning the living room and entering the kitchen. Sara stepped out of the dining area to see what all the commotion was about. Without waiting for a reply, Sam double-timed it up the steps.

"Sam. Sam. What's the matter?" she asked.

Sam could hear Carl saying something to her as he made a beeline for Max's room at the end of the corridor. Upon entering the room, he found Max shrugging on a backpack, and another kid climbing out the window. Before he could get out, Sam latched onto him and dragged his ass back in, tossing him on the floor.

"Whoa man, take a chill pill."

"What the hell were you two playing at?" he yelled.

Sara entered the room, hands outstretched, trying to make sense of the situation and keep everyone calm.

"Would someone tell me what happened?"

Without taking his eyes off Max, Sam responded. "Your son is what happened."

"Look man, I don't have time for this," Max said heading for the window.

Sam grabbed his arm. "I'm afraid you're not going anywhere."

"Get off me, man. You're not a cop anymore."

"No but if I was, I would drag your ass down to the station. You just killed an innocent man tonight."

"Innocent. That's a good one," Eddie said.

"I don't know what you're talking about," Max shot back.

"I know it was you, Max. Don't bullshit me. I saw your face with my own eyes."

Sara got between them. "You need to back up, right now," she said stabbing her finger into Sam's chest. "Right now!" Her mother instinct had kicked in full tilt.

Sam took a few steps back and ran a hand over the back of his neck. "I cannot believe you would be so stupid. So fucking stupid to do what you did."

"It was more than what you two assholes were doing," Eddie chimed in.

Max elbowed him to get him to shut up.

"What is he talking about, Max?"

"I don't know."

"Oh come on. Drop the act." Sam jabbed his finger at them. "You and your buddy showed up at the dock, shot Keith Banning and took that Humvee for a joyride."

"Keith Banning is dead?" Sara asked.

Sam nodded. "Yeah, and…"

Before he could continue any further, Carl appeared in the doorway looking out of breath. "Sam, he's here and he's not alone."

He ran a hand over his face. "Shit."

Sara threw up her hands looking perplexed. "Okay. Look, can someone tell me what is happening here?"

"There's no time. We need to get them out of here and fast."

He strode over to the window and saw flashlights and

several men dressed in military fatigues surrounding the perimeter. "Shit, it's too late." He grabbed Max and thrust him towards the door. "Let's get them up in the attic."

"Sam."

Before he could explain, they heard screaming downstairs and men ordering people to get on the ground. Sam told Carl to prevent them from coming up while he got the two kids out of the way. "Where's the opening to the attic?" he said, his eyes roving the ceiling. Sara pointed to her room.

"It's accessible through our closet."

She led the way and they hurried into her room and used a chair to get the two of them into the attic. "Stay there. No matter what you hear. Don't come out," Sam said closing the closet door and heading towards the stairs with Sara. Before they'd made it to the top, Mick Bennington appeared.

"Where is he, Sam?"

"Who?"

"Don't fuck with me. That boy murdered one of our own." Mick brushed past him and with a nod of the head started having his men search the rooms. "Look, you can make this easy or hard. Tell me where Max is?"

His gaze bounced to Sara. She shrugged. "He went out tonight with a friend."

"Oh I know he was with a friend. I don't know who that other kid was but I will find them. So where are they?"

"You know, you have no right coming here," Sara said. "Where's your warrant?"

"Lady, shut the fuck up," he said walking past her. "Right now you are not in charge. And I don't need a warrant. I am working under the authority of FEMA and the U.S. military."

"More like you are one of their bitches," Carl said coming up the stairs. "This will only end badly if you continue down this path so go easy on her, Mick."

"Down this path?" Mick said turning towards him. "This path was created by her son. Do you see us killing anyone? No. Do you see us taking anyone's weapons? No. And yet you expect me to take it easy? Fuck you. Fuck her. And anyone else who tries to stop us from finding them."

"Hey!" Sam said stepping up to him. "Watch it."

Mick looked him up and down with a smile on his face. "Your time of having authority is over, deputy," he said emphasizing the word deputy. "Step aside or I will forcibly have you removed and arrested."

Downstairs Sam could hear Tess crying. He glanced over the staircase and saw her on the floor with her hands zip tied. The older ones, Janice, Arlo and Rita, were shown some kindness and had their faces pressed against a wall. It was strange to see locals he knew dressed in military fatigues. They were regular folk, hunters, fishermen, but mostly friends of Mick.

"Any luck?" Mick asked.

"Nope."

Mick smiled as his gaze bounced to them.

"We saw them come this way after they dumped the

Humvee in the bay." Mick stepped up to Sam, getting within breathing distance. He could smell alcohol on his breath. "That's right. They not only killed, and stole a Humvee but they destroyed thousands of dollars' worth of government property. So I'm only going to ask this one more time before I arrest all of you. Where is he?"

"We don't know," Sam replied. "Maybe he had second thoughts on coming home."

Mick blew out his cheeks. "All right. Have it your way." He whirled a finger in the air. "Take them in." Suddenly multiple men came at them.

"On what basis?" Sam asked.

"On the basis that you are obstructing justice."

"Hey. Get your hands off me," Sara said struggling before being pushed against a wall and having her wrists zip tied.

* * *

Mick stood back and enjoyed watching as his crew forced them down the stairs and out the door. He turned to Holden. "You checked the other structures?"

He nodded. "What about the attic?"

Both men looked up, their eyes roving the ceiling searching for an opening. Over the next few minutes they went room to room searching for an opening. There had to be one. He knew in older houses it might not be in the same place so they continued until Holden called out to him. "Mick, I've found it."

Mick hurried into the bedroom to find Holden stepping up on a chair and lifting up a panel in the ceiling. It might have seemed like a strange place for an attic for those that were familiar with seeing access doors above the landing, but in his time in Castine, he'd seen a number of homes with access points in the sides of walls, as well as in bedroom closets. Holden hauled himself up and turned on a flashlight and shone it around.

"Anything?" Mick asked from down below.

"Nope. Just boxes."

"Check them."

He waited expecting Holden to find them but after a few minutes he emerged shaking his head. "They're not there."

"Well, perhaps they were telling the truth. Too bad," he said heading out of the room. He figured it was only a matter of time before Max showed his face and when he did they would be there to grab him. He was looking forward to a public hanging. It would send a clear message to anyone else who would try to oppose him.

* * *

Ten, maybe twenty minutes passed before Max moved. There was silence in the house. Max shifted a large panel of wood out of the way and crawled out from the cramped space, reentering the main part of the attic. "For a moment there I thought we were made," Eddie said. "Lucky your dad built this."

"He didn't. I did."

Eddie raised an eyebrow. "Ah, a place to jerk off in silence. Nicely done."

"Oh my God." Max rolled his eyes. "No, I meant I found it. Someone else built this. Previous owner perhaps. It had a dusty old mattress inside, dolls and a bunch of creepy magazines. No idea why it was built and I don't want to know."

"So your parents knew about it?"

"No. Why would I tell them? It was a great place to jerk off in silence," Max said, tossing his words back at him before chuckling. Eddie smirked and hit him on the arm. They quietly made their way down to a small air vent that provided a view of the side of the home. It was too dark out to see if anyone was out there but they couldn't see any flashlights.

"You think they're gone?" Eddie asked.

"Only one way to find out," Max said, making his way over to the attic door. He hesitated to lift it but when he did, he stuck his head down and listened. Nothing. No voices. No footsteps. It was possible they were waiting downstairs but he didn't plan on going down. If they could just get to his room and grab his bag, they could head out the window. "Don't make a noise," he said lowering himself. Eddie followed.

They stopped walking at the sound of a creak. Max

was used to the different sounds that the old house made — groaning water pipes, creaking stairs and wood expanding in hot and wet weather — but that didn't mean he was going to rush to his room. He gave it a minute or two until he was sure no one was there before slowly creeping along the hallway to his room. The second Eddie was inside, he closed the door and they shrugged into their backpacks and headed out the window. A warm breeze blew against his face and the smell of the ocean attacked his senses. Instead of shimmying down to the edge of the roof and dropping to the ground, he climbed up the steep incline to look over the ridge and see if he could make out anyone at the front of the house.

No one.

No vehicles.

No lights.

They were gone. At least he hoped they were.

Carefully they made their way down to the ground then headed for the stable to collect a horse. Max pulled back the door and looked inside but the horses were all gone. "Bastards took them. Shit."

"What did you expect? We took the Humvee." Eddie chuckled. "Anyway, where are we heading?"

He bit down on his lower lip and looked off towards the trees. "To see Ray."

"But you heard what he said."

"I don't give a shit what he said. Right now he's the only one that can help us."

They would have to hike it to Dyce Head. It was less than half a mile away. A short ten-minute walk, five if they jogged it. Aware that Mick's crew were still in the area searching for them, they cut through Witherle Woods and went south parallel to Dyce Head Road.

Even though they were careful not to be seen, staying far back from the road, there were a few times they had to duck behind trees as they saw several of Mick's guys on horseback patrolling the roads and shining their flashlights into the woods. It was all a matter of timing. They waited for their moment and burst out of the forest, crossed the road and worked their way down to the shore. The waves were choppy, splashing against the rocks. A seagull soared overhead squawking. Max retrieved his old fishing boat from its concealed location and under the cover of night they dragged it into the water and hopped in. Eddie took one of the oars and he took the other and they started rowing across the bay to Nautilus Island.

It was close to ten at night when they saw the dock, and were illuminated by blinding light. "Identify yourself."

"It's me. Max Gray. I need to speak to Ray. It's important."

"You're not allowed here. Go home, kid."

"You don't understand. They've taken in my family, Sam, all of them. I shot one tonight, and dumped their Humvee in the bay."

He heard one of them chuckle. "Hold tight." They watched from a distance as the guy got on a two-way radio. A few seconds later the guy waved them in. "You're good. Come on in." Both of them rowed hard the final stretch of the way. As soon as they had their feet on dry land, they hurried up to the house.

Ray was in the middle of a meeting with six others around a table. They were drinking bourbon and smoking cigars when one of his guys led them in. "Ah, Max Gray and his ridiculous sidekick."

"Ridiculous? Fuck you, man," Eddie said.

That only made the men at the table laugh.

"So. I hear you've been causing a storm over on the island. Shot someone. Dumped a Humvee. Tell me more," Ray said leaning back in his seat, intrigued by the tale. Max brought him up to speed. By the time he was done, all of them at the table were no longer smiling. They cast serious glances at one another.

"Arresting American citizens. I knew it would come to this."

"Are you going to help?" Max asked.

"No, kid."

"What?"

"We don't have time for that. We're fighting our own

war."

He turned in his seat and went back to pouring himself a glass of bourbon. Max couldn't believe it. He stared at them.

"Pussies. You know I thought you guys were something else when I heard what you did in Belfast but now I can see you're just a bunch of army wannabes. A cowardly group of assholes."

"Hey! Watch your mouth."

"Why? You're too busy to do anything about it, anyway."

Ray got up and charged at him but Max held his ground expecting him to lash out. He didn't. Ray stared in his eyes and smiled. "Cocky sonofabitch. You remind me of me, doesn't he, Pete?"

"That he does. Except he has a little more hair than you did back then."

They roared with laughter and even Max smiled. Ray placed a hand on his shoulder. "I'm fucking with you, kid. Of course I will help you. I just wanted to see what you're made of. I can see now." He jerked his head towards the table. "Come. Join us."

Chapter 19

Mick cracked Sam on the jaw with such force it knocked him off the chair. With his wrists zip tied behind his back, Sam could do little more than groan and wiggle on the ground. He spat a mouthful of blood before looking up at him with a grin. "Is that all you've got?" A quick jerk of Mick's head and one of his men hauled Sam up again. This time Mick bent at the waist in front of him.

"Ever since you barged into my house and arrested me, I've been looking forward to this day."

Through swollen eyes Sam looked back at him with amusement. "Well get on with it."

Mick sank his fingers into Sam's thighs and stared him in the eye. "Karma has a sick sense of humor, doesn't it?"

Sam chuckled. "That it does."

"Just tell me where the boys are?"

He remained silent.

Mick raised his fist again and Sam finally nodded. "Okay, I'll tell you." He mumbled something and Mick got closer.

"Speak up."

He mumbled causing Mick to get closer.

In an instant, Sam headbutted right on the bridge of his nose with such force it burst like a fire hydrant. Mick stumbled back, groaning and gripping his face. Blood gushed over his lip and dripped off his chin. He clenched his jaw, balled his fists and unleashed a furious flurry of strikes to Sam's face and gut. Every time Sam curled over, Mick had one of his guys drag him up and he continued the assault. In less than five minutes, Sam was barely conscious. Mick spat blood in his face and told his guys to take him back to his cell. He followed them out of the steel housing and watched as Sam's feet dragged behind him, down the narrow corridor inside the ship.

The *State of Maine* was a training vessel used by the Maine Maritime Academy. Every summer more than 250 students and fifty faculty, crew and support staff would board it for its annual training cruise to European ports. This had been the first year it had remained in the dock. Mick was now using it as his main center for operations, and for housing prisoners. The 500-foot, 16,000-ton vessel was perfect with many steel-enclosed rooms in the lower decks, making escape virtually impossible.

One of his guys unlocked a door, and tossed Sam inside with the rest of them. Carl sneered at Mick; his face still swollen from his own beating. The door clanged shut and Mick double-timed it to the upper deck to get an update on the search.

Entering the bridge, he scooped up a cloth and wiped blood from his knuckles before getting on the radio. "Holden, where are you?"

"On the east side of the island."

"Any luck?"

"None so far. We revisited the Manor but no sign of them."

"Well they couldn't have just vanished."

"I'll keep you in the loop."

Mick stared out of the window and then took some binoculars and scanned the tops of the buildings. Anyone brazen enough to shoot one of his guys and steal a Humvee out from underneath their nose might be daring enough to attempt to get his family out. That was another reason why he'd taken them. Still, they needed to get on top of this and fast. There was a lot riding on this first shipment of supplies to FEMA and for a while he was on track to deliver.

What a screw-up.

Now they'd already received word that Colonel Lukeman was planning on paying Castine a visit, what was he meant to do? They had nothing to show for their efforts. All the fish were gone, the Humvee was at the bottom of the bay and they had been outwitted by two teenagers. He still hadn't told Teresa. If she found out, he would be stripped of his position immediately and he hadn't come this far to have the rug pulled out from underneath him. This was the beginning of something big, a means for him to work his way up to a position of power.

Already he had over forty people under his command, and another ten were supposed to sign up. Everything was going to plan. He was making progress until those two assholes screwed it up. Mick turned to Davis, a large, imposing man who used to run his own construction company. "Did you collect the catch this morning?"

"Yeah."

"Fifty percent?"

"That's right."

"We're gonna need more to replace what was taken. Follow me." Mick snatched up his AR-15 and headed out with a group of five. The ship was guarded by ten of his men, and the rest were out searching for the boys. After making their way down a slope to the dock, they got on horses and headed south towards the location where Pete Barnes' company brought in their catch. With fish being the main source of food since the blackout, those who didn't own boats had to give their time and assist in return for a portion of the catch.

Mick pulled on the reins and dismounted, then tied the horse to a post. Locals looked on at the show of force as they emptied nets full of fish into large containers.

"Where's Pete?" he asked one lady.

"On his boat, over there." She pointed. Mick gave some instructions to three of his guys to keep an eye on the people while he went and had a word with Pete. He was only one of a handful of fishermen they would need to approach that morning.

"Pete!" Mick bellowed. Pete looked up from where he was helping a man load crab cages onto the boat. "I need a word with you."

Pete muttered something to his co-worker, hopped off the boat and made his way down the dock, wiping his grimy hands on a rag that he tucked into his back pocket. His clothes were covered in fish guts. He ran a hand over what remained of his hair and frowned as he approached. "Yeah?"

"Walk with me," Mick said turning and clasping his hands behind his back. While he was more than prepared to use force to get his point across, he was of the mind that if he could achieve it without doing so, he stood a better chance of getting the people behind him. It was all a matter of using the right words. He already knew that Pete didn't like him but if he could get him to see it as something that directly affected them all, maybe he could persuade him. "As you know, I have been put in the unfortunate position of assisting FEMA with the collection of supplies. I know you and I haven't seen eye to eye on this matter but understand one thing. If it's not me, they would just find someone else. Either way you would still have to give up 50 percent of your catch."

"But how long do they expect us to do this? We're already spending most of the day out there just to bring in enough for residents, but then they go and take 50 percent and…"

"Pete, I get it. Right now we aren't in a place to negotiate. I was told outright that they would take our guns and our supplies if we didn't contribute."

"Bastards. Just like the government. Greedy. Always

asking for more and yet complaining they don't have enough. You know, they used to take over a hundred thousand dollars from me every year in taxes. I mean, I don't mind paying 10 percent but these guys were taking close to 50 percent and now, finally when the nation goes to shit you think you'll get some relief from their grimy hands, and here they are asking for more. Oh no, they won't come and do the hard work themselves. They expect us to get our hands dirty. Well 50 percent is all they are getting."

Mick sucked air between his teeth. "That's why I needed to talk to you."

"They want more?"

"No they don't, but we're gonna need to take everything you have caught today."

Pete stopped walking and scowled. "What?"

"The Humvee with the previous day's load was taken last night. Dumped in the bay. Everything we had is gone. They are expecting us to deliver today."

Pete laughed. "Then they can keep expecting. That's

not my problem," he said continuing to walk. Mick caught up with him.

"Actually it is. Shit rolls downhill. Now if I fail to deliver they will make good on that promise to take our weapons. Then we will have no recourse if and when things go bad between us and them."

Pete turned fast and jabbed a finger into Mick's chest. "We did what was asked. We're not the ones that screwed up. This is on you, Mick. Not me. Not this community. You! You want to fix this, get out there and fish yourself and hope to God you get enough but we are done."

He turned to walk away and Mick pulled out his revolver and cocked it. "No you're not."

Pete froze. "So this is what it's coming to?"

"I told you. This is not us and you. It's us and them. We are in the same boat together. If I go down, so do all of you. So you are gonna go back to your crew and have them bring all the catch over to our ship. You understand?"

Pete turned slowly, his hands raised ever so slightly. "I

understand you're a bitch."

Mick lunged forward and jabbed him on the nose with the butt of his gun causing his legs to buckle. He went to kick him and Pete caught his leg and swept out the other from beneath him. A scramble for the gun ensued but before Pete could get to it, Davis, one of Mick's men, rushed in and pulled him away while another stuck a gun in his face. "Back off!"

Mick rose to his feet and brushed himself off before putting his gun away. He went over to Pete as a crowd looked on and struck him in the gut twice before pulling up his head by the back of his hair. "If you ever do that again, I will kill you and throw you in the bay. Do you understand?"

Pete gritted his teeth and gave a nod.

"Now you know what to do. Go and do it!"

And just like that they released him and watched him return to his crew where he began barking out orders. They all looked perplexed, and cast a glance at Mick but refused to follow through. Mick unslung his AR-15 and fired off a few rounds over their heads to make sure they knew he meant business. "Now!" he bellowed.

From there he had his men move in and monitor them.

Mick pulled out a rag and wiped his lower lip where Pete had struck him.

His radio crackled.

"Mick, this is Holden, come in, over."

He took the radio off his belt and scowled at the crowd. "Go ahead."

"One of our guys reports seeing the two boys rowing towards Witherle Woods."

"So they were offshore. No wonder." He breathed in deeply. "Bring them in."

"We already have our guys heading over there now."

"Keep me updated."

He breathed in deeply the salty air and smiled. Maybe things were looking up. If they could deliver the load today, and hand over Max and his pal to the military, that would speak volumes for his ability to handle matters.

Sure, the Humvee was gone but he didn't expect them to hold that against him. He got back on his horse and cast one more glance over to Pete, who was busy loading fish into large plastic tubs of ice.

* * *

Sam leaned against the steel wall and looked out of the porthole, trying to see who was shooting. It had been a quick burst of gunfire then it was silent. "You really should sit down," Carl said. "Rest."

"I'll rest when that asshole is dead."

Carl leaned back in a chair and stared up at the ceiling. Tess thumped a fist against the door and asked for the umpteenth time to be let out. "You might as well stop doing that. It's only going to piss them off," Carl said.

"They can't do this," Tess said. "I can't stand it in here. I'm claustrophobic."

"Breathe, honey, just breathe," Rita said trying to calm her nerves.

Sam had to admit it was cramped. It was set up in a bedroom style with one bed, and a tiny closet, but that was it. They'd put them in one of the smallest rooms on the ship and told them they would remain there until they found the two boys at which point they would be released. Janice and Arlo had been placed in a separate room and a couple of times they heard Arlo bellowing at the top of his voice, blaming Sara, but most of all blaming himself for listening to Janice and moving into the inn.

"If we get out of this, I am moving out."

"Settle down, Arlo."

Sam looked over at Sara. She had her knees up against her chest and her arms wrapped around them. For the first few hours she'd been frantic with worry; crying and then getting angry. Eventually she went quiet and withdrew into a corner of the room.

"Penny for your thoughts?" Sam asked, rubbing his aching jaw and taking a seat near her. Two of his teeth had been knocked out. His ribs were so painful it made breathing hard. Every movement was a struggle.

"You don't want to know," she said. "By the way, you look like shit."

"Thanks," he said cracking a smile only to groan as the cut on his lip opened up.

Although he had no idea how they would get out, he tried to remain optimistic. Mick had never been a man for covering all his bases, that's why he'd been arrested numerous times. He reacted then thought later. "He better not harm my son."

"Ah, he's full of hot air. It's all about appearances with him."

"Well it looks like he changed your appearance."

"Yeah, well that's been a long time coming. We have a history."

"I heard," she said, jerking her head towards Carl.

Sam nodded slowly. "Listen, we'll get out of this. I don't know how but we will. Max will be fine. Until then we—"

Pop. Pop. Pop.

Several rounds echoed. Sam rose and went to the window and looked out to see three of Mick's guys lying on the ground. What the hell? Another volley of shots rang out, this time getting louder. He saw another guy drop. The thud of boots could be heard above them. Running. More shots.

"Which one is it?" a voice yelled from outside.

"Please. Don't shoot."

Another two rounds.

"They're in there."

"Tess, back away from the door," Sam said. She took a few steps back and they all heard a key go into the lock, then the door swung open and hope ignited.

Chapter 20

It was a strategic attack.

If he'd only been at the ship when it happened, he might have been able to save face but now he didn't have a leg to stand on. Before receiving word from Holden that his team had been ambushed in Witherle Woods, Mick had taken five of his men to meet Colonel Lukeman and a platoon along Battle Avenue. He'd hoped to delay their arrival so they could ensure the shipment was ready. It would have worked as well. Now he just looked like a chump.

Mick held the radio to his lips. "Holden. Come in. Repeat. What?"

Holden yelled over gunfire, "Men down. Men down! They're on both sides. They've pinned us down in the clearing."

"Who? Where? What?"

Dead. No response.

It was then he'd tried to get in contact with Davis at the boat. No one replied. "Come in, Davis. Davis."

"Problem, Bennington?" Colonel Lukeman asked from the driver's seat of a Humvee. There were two military vehicles behind him.

He raised a finger. "Just give me a minute."

Mick walked away, getting out of earshot, and tried multiple times, hoping that someone would respond. Sweat trickled down his back. He could feel panic creeping up in his chest. No longer able to wait, Lukeman got out of the Humvee and strode over. "You want to tell me what is going on?"

"I'm not getting any response from the ship, and some of my team have been ambushed over at Witherle Woods trying to apprehend two individuals responsible for the death of one of my men."

Lukeman gave him a deadpan expression and shook his head. "Maybe we should have let that deputy handle matters." He turned and pointed for two of the vehicles to head down Main Street toward the dock while he returned to his vehicle and jumped in the driver's side. Mick's group followed on horseback as the Humvee peeled away heading for the woods. As their horses galloped along the edge of the road and they veered into the woods, his heart was racing and his mind worrying more about the consequences for him than the safety of his teams.

A plume of dust kicked up behind the Humvee as it took a hard right by the Manor Inn onto a trail that led into the heart of the woods and to a clearing, the only one that he knew of. They could already see black smoke rising in the distance as they got closer. The smell of fire permeated. As the Humvee burst through the smoke ahead of them, Mick took in the sight of the carnage. It looked as if his entire team had been wiped out. Horses roamed freely. Bodies scattered the ground. He pulled on the reins and dismounted, searching the faces for Holden, one of his closest friends.

No one had been shown mercy. They'd been cut down before some even had a chance to unsling their weapons.

"Holden!" Mick yelled as the colonel's men fanned out, rifles ready to secure the perimeter. From across the clearing he saw Lukeman crouch down over a man. Mick hurried over. "Is it him?"

"No, it's one of the militia. The same group that attacked us in Belfast."

"Militia? But I thought they were working with the National Guard."

Lukeman rose and got on his radio and walked away.

Mick stumbled back as he looked at those he had called friends. He'd known some of them since they were teens in high school. They were good people. Hard working. They didn't deserve this.

He continued his search until he found Holden near the tree line. His gun was nearby and the radio was still in his hand, he'd taken four shots to the back. "Holden," he said turning him over. He clenched Holden's fatigues in his hand and lowered his head. Mick pounded the earth with a fist. In a single moment he'd lost nearly all his team and for what? Seconds turned into minutes. His mind ran amok as he tried to make sense of how this could happen.

Then the radio crackled.

"Come in, Mick."

He looked at the radio. Mick recognized the voice.

"You there, Mick?"

In a flash of rage, Mick snatched up the radio and answered, "I'm gonna kill you."

"Likewise," Sam replied. "Just remember though, you brought this on yourself."

Through gritted teeth he spat back, "On myself?"

"You wanted to be the helm. Now tell me, how does it feel, Mick?"

Mick balled a fist as he rose above Holden and looked out across the clearing at the dead. "If you think this is over, you are mistaken."

Sam never answered.

While waiting for a response, Mick hollered over to Lukeman to find out what the update was on his men who'd headed for the docks. The reply was as expected.

Multiple casualties. Only a couple of his group survived.

"I am going to hunt you down. You hear me, Sam. I'm gonna find you."

There was no answer.

Chapter 21

Unspeakable violence had become normality in a country without power and Landon didn't know what was more horrific, being a victim or bearing witness to the loss of another. He gave a solemn look at Dakota, on her knees, clutching her eight-year-old son's blood-caked duvet which had concealed what was left of his remains.

The smell of decay was unforgettable.

Tears streamed down her cheeks as she let out an almost inhuman guttural cry that only a parent could understand. It echoed in her home offering back no solace. Landon stepped out of the room to give her privacy and beckoned Beth down to the ground floor. It had been a brutal hike covering approximately two hundred and sixty miles along the roughest terrain in order to reach Gorham, New Hampshire — Dakota's hometown. Over two weeks of hiking close to twenty miles a day had worn away at their strength and optimism.

Stepping into the living room, Landon soaked in the disarray: couches turned over, cupboards opened, décor smashed or scattered, family photo frames cracked and blood smeared on walls. Was this what he could expect when he reached Castine? Losing Sara and Max could very well send him over the edge.

Beth crouched and scooped up a photo frame. She blew dust off it and picked out some of the glass before removing the photo. It spoke of a time long before the blackout, when all was right with the world.

"You should leave it where it was," Landon said. "It might upset her."

Beth looked at him then set it back down.

"So what now? I mean what should we do with Dakota?" she asked.

"That's for her to decide."

"Maybe she should come with us."

"We've seen how that worked out last time," Landon replied.

Beth lifted a hand. "Come on. He was a lunatic."

"He also said he was a victim. He wasn't."

"Yeah but we didn't know that."

"We should have known better than to take in a stranger."

"That's what you were," Beth shot back. "And so far that worked out."

"Slightly different."

"How so?"

"Geez Louise, Beth."

He fished into his bag for a map and turned over a chair to take a seat. He flattened it out on his lap and tried to determine the best direction from Gorham to Castine.

"Anyway, I'm gonna ask her," she said.

He looked at Beth. "And I don't get a say in it? What if I don't want her to come?"

Beth put a finger up to her lips. "Keep it down." She strode over to him to keep the conversation quiet. "Then you'll only have to put up with her until we reach

Caratunk."

Landon frowned. "Caratunk? That's northeast, we're heading east."

"I know but to reach Mount Katahdin we'll need to go through Caratunk and Baxter State Park."

"Who said we're going to Mount Katahdin?"

"You did."

He shook his head. "I don't recall saying that."

She shifted from one foot to the next with a look of concern. "Back in North Carolina. You said we would hike the Appalachian."

"Yes. Not all the way."

She widened her eyes and put a hand on her hip. "I told you that my father and I wanted to hike it this year and that I wouldn't get to do it but you said if I came with you we would hike the AT. Landon, I know what you said."

He shook his head in disbelief. "The journey back to Castine from where we were meant going by way of the AT. I didn't say we were going all the way to the mountain. Do you know how far out of the way that is from Castine? It makes no sense. No, look," he said showing her the map and running his finger across it. "We get on US-2, and go from here to Bethel, then Augusta through to Bangor and then on to Castine. By my estimate we are looking at roughly... A hundred and sixty miles, maybe a little more. If we put in twenty miles a day, we'll be there in eight days, give or take."

She slapped the map out of his hand. "That's not what we agreed."

He looked at her dumbfounded. "Beth. I have to get home to my family."

"And I need to reach Mount Katahdin."

"No. You need to stay alive. There is absolutely no reason why we would go out of our way, and spend..." He looked at the map. "Say, twelve or more days reaching the summit, and then have to spend another week to reach Castine. That is stupid."

She stared back at him. "I promised my father I would one day make it there with him. And I'm keeping that promise." She turned to walk away and he got up and grabbed her by the arm.

"No, you're coming home with me."

She yanked her arm away and gave him a stern look. "Don't touch me or tell me what to do. Just as you said... you're not my father. If you want to go to Castine, fine. But I'm going to that mountain with or without you."

"Beth. Just stop and think about this. This isn't a game. Look around you. You've seen how many homes were destroyed. How many towns are overrun with lunatics. You've encountered the crazies on the trail. And yet you want to continue hiking just so you can... what? Say that you made it? You know how stupid that sounds right now? Your father is dead. Gone."

He let his frustration get the better of him.

Her eyes roamed over his face.

"But I'm not," she said. "It might be stupid to you but it means something to me. A promise is a promise. And you made one to me and broke it."

"What? I didn't promise to take you to the mountain.

I said we could hike the AT together. I didn't say until the end."

"So you lied. And after everything I did for you."

"No. Hold on! God. No. I have a family to get back to, Beth. I don't have the time to go traipsing miles out of the way just so you can reach the top of a mountain. And listen, I appreciate all you did but at some point you have to use your noggin and know when it's wise to get off the trail."

"And you think it's going to be any less dangerous in Castine?"

"I don't know. I won't know until I get there," he said.

"And you will. All I'm asking is for a little more time."

He gazed at her, contemplating, and then shook his head. "I don't have more time."

"Then I guess this is where we part ways."

She strode out of the room, and slammed the front door. Landon considered going after her but with the mood that she was in, he thought it would only add fuel to the fire. He groaned as he sank into his seat and glossed over the map again. He shook his head and brought a hand up to his mouth. They'd already traveled hundreds of miles. It made no sense to go north and then head south. He'd be looking at over two weeks before he saw them and that was if nothing untoward happened. History had already proven that the trail was rife with danger. The sooner they got off it and reached Castine, the better. At least there he knew the town, the people and the area. If things were dangerous they could board a boat and head over to one of the many islands.

He looked up and slammed a fist down against the arm of the chair.

Maybe it was time to go their separate ways.

* * *

Hours passed before Dakota reemerged, her eyes swollen from crying. She'd changed out of her previous rags and donned a fresh pair of black jeans, a white undershirt and a wrinkled plaid shirt that looked slightly too big for her. Landon assumed it was her husband's. "Where's Beth?" she asked, wrapping her arms around her chest. Landon turned and gave a strained smile. He rose from his seat and pointed to the window.

"Outside."

Dakota pushed back the drapes letting in a band of warm sunshine. She checked as if needing reassurance that a female companion was still with them. She had yet to tell them what had occurred and he didn't expect it for quite some time. In the weeks on the trail she'd said very few words, and the odd time he or Beth brought up the subject, she would sob hard and they would back off. With her back still turned she just began to open up. "Two months. We had survived that long without an incident." She took a deep breath and lowered her chin while he listened. "Those animals waited until we were asleep before they broke in. It happened so fast. I just remember waking to find a gun pointing at my face. They made me watch as they slit my husband's throat. I was dragged out of the house and they held me while one of them went inside to…" She could barely get the words out. "They killed my little boy. Took his life. He hadn't done them wrong." She looked over her shoulder at him. "I didn't know how he died or if he was even dead as they wouldn't tell me. They seemed to enjoy watching me suffer with the unknown."

"That was the first time you laid your eyes on him since you left?"

She nodded.

"What was his name?"

"Thomas." She got all choked up again but managed to keep herself from breaking down. She'd already drained the well of tears. There was a long period of silence. Landon joined her at the window. Outside Beth rocked gently back and forth on a porch rocker, her feet up on the wraparound railing, a rifle on her lap at the ready.

"Do you have any other family?" Landon asked.

"My sister is in California. My parents passed away before the blackout."

He nodded, his eyes shifting from left to right down Bangor Road. Across the street they saw someone dart out of a home with a bag and race into the surrounding forest. They weren't the only ones trying to survive. Although they'd had a bad experience with Billy, he got a sense that Dakota was just in an unfortunate situation. Perhaps fate had played a role in their paths crossing, or this was another test by life in trusting a stranger. He decided to roll the dice. "Look, Dakota. I'm heading for Castine, it's about an eight-day hike from here. Beth wants to go to Katahdin and complete the AT but umm—"

"I heard you," she said, shooting him a sideways glance.

"You did?"

"The floors are thin and the vents always carried our voices." She took a deep breath and closed her eyes. Was she thinking of family? Reliving a memory? All of them were tarnished by the past. They were broken individuals trying to do what was right even if at times it had led them to make decisions that had landed them in hot water.

"You are welcome to come to Castine with us."

"Sounds like Beth has other plans."

He scoffed. "Beth is strong-willed. It's probably why we've survived this long. I've never met a girl like her." He snorted and looked out. "I really would have liked to have met her father."

"You know, she still needs a father," Dakota said, pausing for a second before continuing. "Even if she won't admit it." She looked at him. "You're probably the closest thing to that. What she did for you on that mountain, that has got to be worth something."

He closed his eyes and sighed. "Yeah. I mean, of course it is but…"

"Can you predict it will be any safer going your way?"

"No but—"

"Then what's an extra few days on the trail going to matter?"

Landon exhaled hard and ran a hand over his face. "I don't know. It's been so long since I've seen my family and…"

"You miss them. I understand. So does she. This hike to complete the AT means a lot to her. I'm not going to tell you what to do, Landon, as I'm still unsure myself but give it some more thought." She turned and went to walk out of the room. "I'm going to collect a few things before we head out."

"So you're leaving?"

"With Beth. Yeah."

He nodded slowly. Dakota went back upstairs and he looked out the window and sighed before joining Beth on the porch. She looked at him for a second and then turned away as he took a seat beside her. There was silence for a minute or two before he said, "Do you know there are very few people I have spent time with as long as you? I mean — in hours, days, weeks, even months. You've taught me a lot about myself. My weaknesses. My strengths. Hell, this entire journey has been one big learning experience. We've come a long way. I guess Castine can wait an extra week."

"Really?" she asked in a surprised way. "So you're

coming with me?"

"Yes, no, I mean — you are going with me, as I promised." He paused and clarified further. "Though I don't recall saying I would take you all the way to Katahdin, but nevertheless. Why not? The reality is I shouldn't even be here right now. And…" He sighed. "I think it's what Ellie would have wanted me to do."

"Smart girl," she replied, her lip curling.

"Yep, reminds me of someone else," he said, smiling as he tapped her leg.

Chapter 22

Reaching Caratunk had one massive watery hurdle — the Kennebec River, a strong, 170-mile long, 70-yard wide river that split the state of Maine in two, snaking down from the northern region of Moosehead Lake to the Gulf of Maine. The first sign of its existence was the powerful sound. The forest dissolved before Landon, opening into a clearing where grassy banks rolled into the rushing waters. They'd come across many water crossings along the AT, but they all paled in comparison to the Kennebec. With a dam and hydroelectric generation plant, the depth and speed of the current could change in a matter of minutes but even with the power out it looked daunting.

"Where's the bridge?" Landon asked, cupping a hand over his eyes and scanning the river.

"Between Richmond and Dresden, though there is also one between Bath and Woolwich," Beth replied without hesitation as she dumped her backpack down and rolled her head around to work out tension in her shoulders.

Landon screwed up his face. "But that's…"

"About ninety miles south. Yeah, I know what you're about to say, Landon, but people have forded this river successfully before."

"Forded? You expect us to ford across this river?"

"Actually I wasn't expecting that… most hikers use the ferry. A canoe ferry, I mean."

He squinted. "Where's the canoe?"

She swallowed hard and pointed. "On the other side."

Dakota had been a little slower at keeping up with them but Grizzly had stayed back with her to make sure nothing happened. She emerged from the forest with a smile on her face and exclaimed, "Wow, that's beautiful."

"The other side? The other side!" Landon shrugged off his backpack and threw it down hard. "When I agreed to go with you I didn't expect to find myself facing this."

"You're from Maine. Surely you would have known about this."

"I'm from Florida. The only section of Maine I have traveled in is the eastern side. I haven't really been farther than the county."

"It's common knowledge, isn't it, Dakota?"

"The Kennebec River. Yeah," she said, her eyes bouncing between them with a look of confusion as to what she'd walked into.

"Oh well thank you for that valuable insight." He huffed.

"Look, if I knew you were going to be such a baby about it, I would have headed north and used the bridge at Forks, or south to the Wyman Dam but that would have taken us even longer, and you said you didn't have time."

Landon threw his hands in the air. "I meant to hike north. Had I known about this I would have looked at what our options were."

"There aren't many!" she said trying not to lose her patience. "Those who hike the AT go this route and use the canoe ferry. A few brave souls ford the river. But that's uncommon nowadays."

"The canoe?"

"Yeah."

"Which so happens to be on the eastern side of the river, Beth. We're on the west."

Her brow furrowed. "Like I didn't already know that."

He blew out his cheeks. "Well we can't ford this river."

"Give me one reason why not?"

"I'll give you three. Hypothermia. The current. And…"

"And?"

He gritted his teeth. "Alright. I don't know how to swim," Landon said.

"What?"

"You heard me. I never learned."

"But you live by the water."

"You don't have to remind me."

"You don't have to swim. You walk through this. It might come up to your chest in a few areas but you mostly have your feet on the stones," Beth said.

"And get soaked."

"We'll dry our clothes on the other side."

"And the guns?"

"Hold them above your head."

"While I try to not lose my footing on the slimy rocks beneath the water. Right, yeah, that's a good idea, Beth." He looked at Dakota, hoping she might side with him. "What about you?"

She shrugged. "I can swim."

"I didn't ask if you could. I'm asking, do you feel okay with this?" Now he felt a complete fool. A man afraid of bugs, now water. He groaned.

"Well, it's not ideal but like she said unless you want to hike north or south for another…" She waited for Beth to fill in the details.

"About five hours south, two and a half north. However to use the northern bridge you would still have to ford another river as the Kennebec forks with Dead River."

He chuckled with a frown. "Of course it does." He

clenched a fist. "Fuck!"

"Look, I don't see the problem. So we get a little wet. The dam isn't in operation so the current should be fine."

He pointed to the river where the water was rushing. "Does that look fine?"

Beth scooped up her backpack and shrugged into it. "Okay. We do it your way. We'll hike south to the dam. It's going to take another five hours but hey, at least you don't have to get wet." She strolled past him and he stood there gritting his teeth. Dakota raised an eyebrow at him and looked at Beth who had already reached the tree line.

"Okay. I will do it," Landon said.

Beth stopped walking and looked back.

"Oh no, don't worry. I don't mind walking another fifteen miles, though it will be dark by the time we reach there and…"

"Beth, just come back before I change my mind," he said.

She got this smirk on her face as she strolled back. "For what it's worth I thought the canoe would be on this side, or…"

"Just forget it."

"Look, I'll ford across the river, bring the canoe over and then you don't have to get wet."

"And what if the current takes you downstream?"

"Then I'll cling to a tree and make my way back up."

"If you can reach it."

"Landon, please, would you stop thinking negatively. We are where we are. Let me handle this. Stay here with Dakota and I'll go across."

"I'll go with you," Dakota said.

"No, there's no point. I'll come back once I get over. Besides, you can hold Landon's hand so he doesn't worry," she said with a smile on her face.

Landon flipped her the bird and she burst out laughing.

"Okay," Dakota said, shrugging off her backpack and sitting down on top of it. A bright morning sun shone down on them as Beth removed her pants to avoid resistance and left them with her bag. She then selected a spot along the bank to wade into the rushing water and used a large branch to offer some support as she made her way out.

"Brave girl," Dakota said.

"You haven't seen the half of it," he said cupping a hand over his eyes and laying back to watch Beth angle herself upstream so the current would pull her down a little bit. That way she could avoid fighting the current versus going directly across and feeling it tugging her farther downstream.

Dakota squinted. "So you said you have a wife and son?"

He glanced at her, taking his eyes off Beth for just a moment. "That's right. Max. He'll be eighteen by the time I get home." He smiled. "I miss him."

"And Ellie."

"The daughter I lost."

"I'm sorry."

He felt a heaviness press down on his chest at the mention of her name.

"You been married long?"

"A long time. Yeah." He looked back and saw Beth making progress. It was slow but she was steadily wading across the watery expanse.

"Mike and I were married six years."

Landon wasn't sure what he was supposed to say. He didn't want to upset her as it was all still fresh and yet on the other hand maybe talking about them was therapeutic. Everyone dealt with death in different ways. Some would close up, retreat and say nothing, others would go on and act like nothing had happened. The rest would have good and bad days. He knew she had at least a month to chew over her husband's death as well as her son's but seeing his remains must have felt like a scab being torn off an old wound.

"How have you coped since losing Ellie?"

That was the first time someone had asked. Beth avoided the topic as she knew it meant discussing her father and that was just as painful.

He kept his eyes on Beth as he replied. "I try not to

think about it."

Dakota nodded. "I'm wondering when this heavy feeling will lift."

"Well, for me it's been almost seven months since it happened and the pain is still there."

Finally Beth reached the other side and she waved to them before making her way down to a red canoe that was tied to a small wooden dock. How it had survived all this time without being taken was anyone's guess but he was just pleased that one thing was going right. Beth untied it and stepped into the boat and stood up to paddle it over.

"It must feel good to know you aren't that far away from home."

Landon offered back a strained smile. He was elated and yet overwhelmed by the thought of informing his family of Ellie's death. His lack of response ended the conversation. Beth hollered to them from about thirty feet away. "See. It was a piece of cake."

"All right, smartass," he said rising to his feet and

making his way down to grab the nose end of the boat. Beth jammed the one paddle into the stones in the shallow water and hopped out as Landon held the canoe while Dakota and Grizzly got in and took a seat at the far end. Dakota slipped into a faded orange life jacket and handed one to him. Meanwhile Beth tossed the paddle down on the rocks near her bag and went about drying herself off and getting back into her pants. "Hurry up, I can't hold this all day," Landon said as he juggled to hold it with one arm and slip into the life jacket with his other.

"Impatient. Just get in, I'll be there in a second."

"You know you have a hole in your underpants," he remarked.

Beth put her hands on her ass and Landon roared with laughter.

"He's joking," Dakota said, giving him a slap on the shoulder as he got into the canoe and put his arm through the other portion of the life jacket. The whole thing felt very bulky. The water was moving fast at that time of day. Even with the canoe's nose slightly up on the shore, the back end was being shoved hard by the strong current.

Landon turned to calm Dakota.

Beth had one leg in her jeans when Dakota screamed, "Beth. Watch out!"

Landon cast a glance over his shoulder just in time to see a fresh-looking Billy rear back the paddle and strike Beth in the face. She buckled and was knocked unconscious. Grizzly barked loudly and tried to get out of the canoe, making it even more unstable. Billy pulled a handgun just as Landon went for the rifle lying in the canoe. "Ah! I wouldn't do that," he said pointing the gun at him. "And you better get a grip on that dog or else." Landon's gaze bounced between him and a very unconscious Beth who was lying face down on the pebbly shore. Dakota gripped Grizzly's collar tightly. Billy made his way down to the edge of the water and put his foot up on the nose of the canoe. "Throw the rifle into the water. Do it! Now!" he bellowed. He looked a lot better than when they last saw him. Landon reached down. "Slowly. Slowly!" he said. Could he have managed to grab up the rifle and shoot him before he got a shot off? Doubtful. One glance at Billy's finger on the trigger of his handgun and that idea went out the window. Landon tossed the rifle into the water.

"And the handgun."

He gritted his teeth as he did the same again. The water splashed and he watched it sink.

"You don't have to do this," Landon said. "Take whatever you want."

"I intend to," he said, a smile forming. He gave a nod to Dakota. "And who might you be?"

"Leave her alone."

He chuckled. "Oh… the great hero. You were lucky last time. Do you know how long I've been waiting for this? I could have shot you but that would have been too easy. Then I saw you pick up this beauty. The longer I waited, the more exciting it got. Every day it was fun to watch you look over your shoulder. There were a couple of times I was sure you saw me. But, you didn't. Then this presented itself and I heard how scared you are of water. A grown ass man can't swim." He tutted.

"If you're gonna kill me, just pull the fucking trigger."

"Oh, I'm not gonna kill you, Landon. The river will do that."

Billy forcefully shoved the canoe away from the shore and the strong current sucked it out into deep waters. He then held his gun low and fired three shots at the canoe. Water began pouring in and panic crept up in Landon's chest. His eyes widened and darted between the canoe filling with water, and Billy smiling and giving him a military salute before hurrying over to Beth and dragging her towards the forest. "No. No!" he yelled. Trying to scoop out water, seeing Billy drag Beth away and realizing that the canoe was heading downstream fast — it was all too much for his mind to handle.

"We've got to get out," Dakota said.

"I can't swim," he replied as he frantically scooped water out.

"You have no choice."

Within seconds the canoe had taken in so much water

that the front end was beginning to sink. "Give me your hand," Dakota said.

"What?"

"Your hand!"

She clamped on to it and rolled out into the water. Landon's eyes widened as he took a deep breath and went under. He came up gasping only to find himself going back under again. All the while as they were dragged downstream, he could still feel Dakota gripping his hand. Out the corner of his eye he saw Grizzly then he vanished. The frigid waters made it hard to breathe and every few seconds he would find himself gulping water. If she hadn't grabbed him under the arms and begun to scissor kick back towards the shore, he was certain he would have drowned. "Kick your legs. Kick!" she bellowed as they fought against the current and tried to make it to the shore. Using every ounce of strength he had, he kicked until suddenly he felt rocks beneath him. He placed his feet down. Coughing and spluttering they crawled out of the water and collapsed on the bank, exhausted. Landon coughed up water and inhaled fast.

"Slow your breathing," Dakota said turning over onto her back. He drew up his knees and whipped his head around to see where they were.

One look and it was clear they had traveled a fair distance downstream.

"Grizzly!"

Farther down he saw the dog crawl out of the water, and shake off. The relief was short-lived. Not only were they several miles downstream, soaking wet, without backpacks or weapons but they were now on the other side of the river.

"Beth!" he bellowed but his voice was lost in the harsh wind.

Chapter 23

Blood rushed to her head as it bounced lightly against something firm. Building pressure, droplets of blood, she felt sick. The world was upside down when her eyelids fluttered open. The foul stench of body odor, her nose pressing into a shirt, her head throbbing and stomach aching from being bent over — a shoulder? She was being carried and her wrists were tied. An influx of memories: wading across the river, rowing a boat, Dakota screaming and then… Billy. Fear shot through her. He coughed hard and stopped and lowered her to the ground. *Think fast.* She closed her eyes and pretended she was still unconscious. Her body slumped to one side and she heard him humming a tune as he walked a short distance away.

Through slitted eyes she watched as he gathered together some branches, snapped them and tossed them into a pile. She spotted the revolver at his hip. Her hand slid down to her waist hoping to find her own but it was gone, as was the knife. Damn it. She knew her best chance of survival wasn't to fight but to run. But that relied on timing. One wrong move and she could find herself with a bullet in the back.

Beth waited.

Billy looked over and she kept her eyes shut.

She heard him come over and crouch. He pushed her hair back behind her ear and muttered, "I know it's going to take some time but you'll eventually enjoy being with me." He lowered his face and kissed her cheek. "So soft." Inwardly she grimaced, wanting to lash out, but she remained still. He got up and walked away. She watched through slitted eyes as he trudged out of the clearing and disappeared into the brush.

This was it.

Beth's eyes snapped open.

She jumped up only to collapse immediately and let out a groan.

Looking down at her boots she saw that he'd tied the

laces together.

Bastard.

A sudden burst of laughter and Billy reappeared with an armful of branches.

"Oh that was priceless. Run, little mouse. Run." He laughed harder.

She didn't even bother to attempt to untie them as there had to be at least ten tight knots. Billy dumped the branches and Beth scrambled back against a tree as he strode over with a glint in his eye. "Now why would you want to run?"

"Where's my dog, and Landon?"

"Probably at the bottom of the river or miles downstream. Either way they're not coming to save you this time. And besides, do you really want to be saved?"

He crouched in front of her but kept a good distance. She wanted to spit in his face but that would have only got a reaction. She had to play this smart. Billy continued, "I nearly died out in that forest that night. I spent a long time following. At first I wanted to kill you both but then

I thought about it. It was him not you that had a problem with me." Billy put a finger up to her head and tapped her temple. "You see, he got in there and messed with your mind but don't worry, I'll put it right." He curled his fingers and stroked her cheek. "You and I. We've got something special. And now we're together again we'll have a lot of fun. You'll see." He stared intently at her then quickly turned away and just like that he was back to acting normal. "I was about to cook some breakfast. You want some? Squirrel. I hope you don't mind. I ran out of supplies but we should be able to replenish them at the next town."

She nodded. "Yeah, I'm a little hungry." Beth had decided to play along. If her time with Dakota had taught her anything, it was that the only way she'd stayed alive all that time on the trail was by giving those lunatics the impression that they were in control. Then it was just a matter of time. Billy would let his guard down, trust her and when he wasn't looking she'd turn the tables.

As he started a fire, she thought of Landon and felt an

ache in her chest.

Was he dead? Dakota too?

Probably. He wouldn't have made the mistake a second time.

She tried to slip her feet out of the boots but he'd made sure they were secure.

"You want to hear a song? I just came up with it," he said. "Oh, and check out this new banjo of mine. You guys destroyed the other one so I got one while you were in Pawling." He scooped up his instrument and began strumming while singing some horrendous tune with a voice that sounded so bad she would have preferred to listen to nails being raked down a chalkboard. "What do you think?" he asked. "It's still a little rough but I think it has potential. Hell, maybe if the power comes back on I could send it in as a demo. You know, I've always wanted to get a record deal and play big venues but…" His brow furrowed as he stared at her. "You didn't like it, did you?"

"No. I loved it. The dynamics. The subtle nuances. You really do have a gift."

"You're just saying that, aren't you?"

"No. You really do."

She wanted to smash that banjo over his head and ram the fretboard down his throat. Now that would have been a sweet sound.

"Ah thanks. I'm working on another. I'll let you hear it after breakfast."

She pursed her lips and gave a nod. "You know these boots are kind of tight."

"Sorry about that but it's only for a while. Just until I can trust you. Can't have you running off. Besides, it's dangerous out there. You never know who you might bump into." He got this sly grin on his face then turned back to the fire. He placed a thin grill over the rocks and charred wood, and then began skinning a squirrel. "The squirrel might be a little tough as I've had it a few days. But I hope you like it." Beth wanted to scream but instead she tipped her head back and said a silent prayer.

* * *

"Are you crazy?!" Dakota said thrusting a hand against

Landon's chest to prevent him from going into the water. "I just pulled you out. You're not going back in."

"I'm not leaving her behind."

"No one is expecting you to. I can go."

"Out of the question."

"What, because you think I'm not strong enough?"

"Oh please, Dakota, get out of the way. I don't have time for this."

Again she forced herself in front of him. "Even if you make it across, which I highly doubt you will, what then? What can you do? You have no weapon and he has a gun. Besides, they could be anywhere by now."

"I'll take Grizzly. He'll find her."

"And risk his life too?"

"You don't know him like I do."

She shook her head. "Then I'm going with you."

"No. Stay here."

"You don't get to decide," she said walking upstream. "If we're going across we need to find a shallower place." Dakota cursed loudly as Landon beckoned Grizzly to follow. Soaking wet, water sloshing around in their boots, they trudged over the stony shore heading north for several miles until they came across the dock that the canoe had originally been tied to.

Landon squinted and saw the red paddle on the other side. "Okay. I can do this," he said. He waded knee deep into the water and the same fear that had gripped him when he was going under crept over him. Focus, focus, he told himself.

"You got Grizzly?" Dakota asked. He could see she was pissed off and he understood but Beth had gone to hell and back for him and he couldn't look himself in the mirror if he left her behind. This wasn't about being a hero, it was about doing the right thing, and doing what he couldn't do for his own daughter. He kept a firm grip on the dog's collar as they waded out into the depths. So far so good. The water came up to his waist and he was managing to stay upright. Grizzly was in a full doggy paddle beside him and Dakota tried to stay to the side of him in order to take the bulk of the current.

There were only a couple of times he slipped on the rocks and thought he'd be swept away but Dakota grabbed him in both instances. "Don't you go drifting off," she said as water sprayed in their faces.

Soon it was up to his chest and that's when he really started to feel the resistance. He was just waiting for the ground to drop but it never did. "Keep going!" Dakota yelled as his legs grew tired and he slowed.

Slow and steady, that was the rhythm.

Eventually the water lowered until it was up to his knees. A surge of confidence beyond what he'd felt before gripped him. He sped up, water sloshing around him as he made it through the final stretch. As soon as they were on the shore, Grizzly shook his body, and Landon took a moment on his knees to catch his breath. He looked back at where they'd come from and marveled at the achievement.

He removed his boots and poured the water out before sinking his cold feet back inside. It was one of the most uncomfortable feelings ever.

"You good?" Dakota asked.

He nodded.

Dakota went over to Beth's backpack which was still where she'd set it down and fished inside hoping to find a gun, but there was nothing except clothes, the tent, a small medic kit, and a sleeping bag rolled up beneath the pack.

"I have an idea," he said. Landon staggered over to the wooden paddle and smashed the end against the rocks until it cracked and he was able to break off a section of the wooden blade at the end to fashion a long, thick jagged spear. Following suit, Dakota rummaged in the nearby tree line for a thick branch that she could snap and use as a weapon. Both would have been useless against a gun but the handgun was only useful if he saw or heard them coming.

Taking a piece of clothing from Beth's bag, he placed it against Grizzly's nose. "That's it, boy, find her. Find Beth." They took off into the woods more determined than ever.

* * *

Back at the small camp, dark black smoke swirled up into the air above the fire Billy had created. It was laughable. He had zero positional awareness. Beth had always been careful to avoid creating fires. The times she did create them she opted for what was known as a Dakota pit — a simple design used by the military, it relied on digging two small pits in the ground connected by a vent. By keeping the fire below ground it provided the added benefit of hiding the flame, and then when they needed to move on they could just cover it over with sod.

Billy thrust his grubby fingers into Beth's mouth. She bit down on the squirrel meat that was undercooked. "Tastes good, doesn't it?" She felt like gagging but instead she nodded with enthusiasm.

He set the pot down and pulled out a half-smoked cigar from his pocket and scurried over to the fire like some strange creature. Once it was lit, he blew out gray smoke and smiled at her. "You want some?"

"I'm good, thanks. You wouldn't have some water, would you?"

"Sure." While his back was turned she went back to tugging her feet apart and trying to use one boot to push off the other one. She'd already managed to loosen the laces by rubbing the tip of her foot against them. It was tricky at first but the more she tugged, and scraped her toes against them, the weaker the laces became. She didn't expect them to break but she was hoping she could loosen the boot. As soon as he turned she stopped and smiled back. He returned and brought a canister to her lips. "You know you have pretty lips," he said.

"Thank you."

It was so hard to restrain her disgust for him.

The thought of what the night would bring if she didn't get out of these boots lingered at the forefront of her mind. "You know, when we were traveling together I used to watch you while you washed in the river."

Okay, that couldn't be any more creepy, she thought.

"I know you're younger than me but age is just a

number, right?"

She wanted to throw up in her mouth.

"Right?" he fished for an answer.

Beth shrugged. "I guess."

He took another toke on his cigar and his lips formed a smile. "I was thinking we could go back to Pawling. You remember all the resources they had."

"You were there?"

"Of course I was. It was hard to remain out of sight but it's amazing what you learn when you have no other option. Anyway. Now that you know that lady. What was her name?"

"Abigail."

"That's it. Abigail." He squinted. "You could tell her that you changed your mind. Landon continued on his way and you met up with your boyfriend. Me. Ah, you'll get used to it. What do you think?" He fished his fingers into the pot and scooped out more squirrel and offered it to her. She declined, so he opened his mouth and dropped it in.

"Sounds like a plan."

He leaned forward and ran his hand around her face. "See. We're already off to a good start. Right, well I'm gonna clean up and…"

"You wouldn't have any fruit, would you?"

"An apple. Would that do?"

"Perfect."

Once again as he turned, she worked away at her boot with the other foot, until she suddenly felt the boot slip. Billy turned back before she could get her foot out so she just remained still, waiting for him to come over and feed her. He rubbed the red apple against his chest and rattled on about the future and how it was fate that she crossed his path. "Here you go," he said crouching and bringing the apple to her mouth.

She took a large bite. "Oh that is good," she said.

He took a bite. "You're right."

Meanwhile she managed to slip her left foot out of her boot.

"Another bite?" she asked trying to distract him and

make sure he didn't notice while she used her free foot to push the other boot off. Running in socks wasn't uncommon to her. Growing up on the mountain she had spent the better part of her childhood running around with no shoes or socks on.

"One more and then we must move on. I can't have—"

Before he got the next word out, Beth reared back her leg as fast as possible and thrust it into his nutsack, then followed through with another to the face. It all happened within seconds. Beth bounced up, her wrists still tied, and took off into the forest. She had no idea where she was, only that she had to put as much distance as possible between her and him. She hit the ground running, threading around trees, stumbling and having sharp rocks jab into her feet. Every direction looked the same. Her thighs burned as she heard Billy scream her name. "Beth!"

She struggled to control her panic, fear getting the better of her.

While she figured he might not kill her —

punishment, that was definitely in the equation. It was the crack of his gun that changed all that. Beth felt like a hunted animal. Her mind went into overdrive.

"I trusted you, Beth."

Beth was so preoccupied by looking over her shoulder to see if he was catching up or about to shoot her that she didn't see what lay ahead. Her foot caught on a downed log and she stumbled over into the underbrush and the ground disappeared beneath her. Like a rock bouncing down a hill, she twisted and turned and spun out of control down a steep incline while flattening plants, brambles and tall grass until she collided with a tree trunk.

She let out a muffled cry. Cut and bruised, she was sure she'd broken a rib or two. Every breath was harder than the last.

Get up… you need to move… Rattled, she crawled onto her belly and clawed at the soil until she was back on her feet. That's when she heard him.

"You won't survive out here, Beth. Come out."

Beth scrambled behind a boulder and pressed her body against it and slowed her breathing. Only the sound of Billy's voice could be heard. She looked down at her arms and hands that were cut up. Blood was trickling down her arm and she realized there was a piece of a branch embedded. She clamped on to it and gritted her teeth then pulled it out. The pain was agonizing. She closed her mouth and tears welled in her eyes. Beth dropped the bloody piece of wood and scanned the ground for a stone, anything she could use as a weapon. Dropping to her knees she dug out a rock the size of a baseball and held it tightly as Billy's voice got louder. He was almost upon her.

Exhausted, in pain and bleeding badly, she knew if she didn't face him, he'd keep coming after her and she would bleed out. A surge of anger and pure will drove her out from her hiding spot and up the incline. She yanked on tree roots and thick underbrush to reach the cusp of the ridge she'd gone over. Between the trees she saw him. He kept looking around and wheeling the gun in a crazy fashion. She knew the odds were against her but with Grizzly, Landon and her family gone, she had nothing else to lose.

Darting over to a tree, she crouched down waiting for him to walk by. A quick peek. He wasn't heading her way. *Damn it.* She rushed to the next tree, then the next and it was when she sprinted for a boulder that a dark mass came out of nowhere, nothing but a blur before she was dragged down.

Beth struggled, automatically thinking it was Billy.

"Stay silent."

"Landon?"

Chapter 24

The reunion was short-lived. Keeping a firm grip on Beth, he eyed Billy in the distance. He had his back turned. "Okay, listen to me. Dakota is about half a mile from here." He pointed. "Head that way and she'll see you."

"What about you?"

"He'll keep coming if I don't end him."

"But Landon."

"For once. Please. Just do as I say."

She studied him for a second or two then nodded, and while Billy was still searching the forest, Landon released her and she took off running, staying low and out of sight. Landon saw the cuts and bruises on her. He could only imagine what he'd done to her. Rage bubbled up inside as he tightened his grip on the spear. He held it with both hands and waited for his moment before bursting from tree to tree to get closer. He couldn't risk throwing it. He'd have to get close which meant increasing the odds of being shot. Billy already had a gun in his hand, and his finger on the trigger.

"Beth! You're starting to piss me off," Billy roared turning 360 degrees and firing a few random rounds into the forest as if that would motivate her to come out of hiding. What an idiot.

Figuring it was better to have Billy come to him than risk him hearing his approach, Landon crouched down and took a stone the size of his hand and tossed it about fifteen feet away. The rock hit a tree, then rolled down through the brush. Billy whirled around, a smile spreading as he broke into a jog holding his handgun out in front of him. Landon slid his body around the tree and waited. He eyed the ground below him. There was the smallest amount of brush at his feet. Would he hear him? It was a risk he would have to take. This was the closest he could get without being spotted.

"I know you're out there," Billy said, his voice so loud that it sounded as if he was right beside him. Landon snuck a peek around the tree and saw Billy peering over the rise down the grassy slope. His hands began sweating and his throat went dry. He rubbed them together and then readjusted his grip.

This was it.

Now or never.

Without a cry, Landon wheeled around and burst forward, his spear out like an Olympic pole vaulter making their approach. His thighs punched the ground like pistons. Billy's head turned, his eyes widened and instinctively he brought up the handgun but it was too late. Landon thrust the spear into his side with such force that both of them went over the rise and rolled down the slope. Crashing through the underbrush, their bodies collided and bounced off each other like balls in a pinball machine.

At some point, Landon must have cracked his skull against a rock as when he awoke his head was throbbing, and there was blood dripping onto his hand. He groaned and drew up his knees beneath him, immediately checking his body to see if he'd been shot. No. Everything was in order. His bones hurt like hell but he was alive and in one piece. Quickly he scanned the terrain for Billy, unsure of how long he'd been out. Turning fast he scrambled over to a nearby tree seeking cover until he could figure out where Billy was. He heard groaning but couldn't place where it was coming from. The sound seemed to bounce off the wide trees.

Then.

He saw movement.

Billy was scrambling up the slope, one hand gloved in blood as it pressed against his rib cage. In the other was the handgun. He turned, surveyed and saw Landon. He fired off two rounds in his direction, one lanced the tree, the other tore up the dirt. He knew he couldn't let him escape. And that was exactly what Billy was trying to do. Dealing with tremendous pain, Landon had to dig deep to find the strength to blast away from the tree and shorten the distance between them.

Another round echoed.

Every time he darted out it was like playing Russian roulette with his life.

Billy lost his footing and stumbled and rolled back down the slope. He cried out in pain but was quick to get back up and fire off a few more rounds. How many did he have left? Landon spotted the bloodstained spear nearby. He raced over to it, scooped it up and darted from one tree to the next, and then took cover behind a mossy boulder.

"I should have killed you," Billy yelled.

Landon never replied. A few times he tried to sneak a peek, and Billy unloaded a few more rounds. "You're running out of bullets, Billy," Landon shouted. He shot out again, playing with fate. Landon zigzagged his way through the trees getting closer by the second. Billy clawed his way up the slope, nervously looking back and firing shots until there was no more ammo. Landon knew it as he heard him curse and toss it.

That's when he stepped out and looked at him.

"Look, we can work this out," Billy said.

Landon said nothing as he strode towards him with only one thing on his mind.

Billy backed up but stumbled again, his hands hidden by the brush which he clung to as he tried to avoid slipping down.

"You're losing blood fast," Landon said as he got closer.

"Please. Just leave me to die."

Within spitting distance, Landon replied, "You made that mistake with me, I won't." With that said, Landon thrust the spear at him only to have Billy lunge forward drawing a knife hidden behind underbrush. They struck each other at the same time. The spear penetrated Billy's sternum and his knife drove into Landon's lower abdomen. Their eyes widened. Landon staggered back, clutching his side, as Billy collapsed and blood streamed over his lips.

Landon dropped to his knees; his breath stuck in his throat.

He didn't take his eyes off him for even a second.

Only when Billy took his last breath did Landon lay back and stare up at the blue sky. Clouds melted; others passed overhead. Birds chirped and the wind rustled leaves.

In that moment he wasn't scared or fearful of dying.

It was peaceful.

"Wake up. Wake up," a familiar voice said.

His eyes fluttered and there standing over him was Ellie.

Was he dead?

"Ellie?"

"Hi, Dad," she said in a soft tone.

"Baby." Tears welled in his eyes; his chest became heavy.

"You need to wake up," she said.

"But…"

"WAKE UP!" the voice changed from soft to harsh.

In an instant, Ellie was gone and Beth was looming over him. "Wake up!" He coughed a few times. "Oh my God, I thought you were gone. Don't you ever do that to me." Tears streamed down her cheeks. Out the corner of his eye he saw Grizzly and Dakota. His hand reached up and the knife was gone. In its place was a bunched-up shirt. Beth was applying pressure.

"How long, Beth?" Dakota asked.

"Ten, maybe fifteen minutes of direct pressure should be enough to control the bleeding." Landon noticed his body had shifted, his head was now facing down the slope and his legs higher up. He knew from the little knowledge he had of knife wounds that if the wound was below the heart, blood loss would occur faster and so to offset that, repositioning the wound above the heart slowed it down.

"Dakota," Beth said tossing her the blood-soaked shirt. Dakota handed her another piece of clothing. Neither one looked sanitary but it was better than nothing. Beth shook a canister of water over the wound and he winced in pain before she covered it.

"What about infection?" Dakota asked.

"Not many options right now," she said. "Hang in there, Landon."

"You gotta stop making this a habit," he said managing to form a smile.

"What?"

"Saving my ass."

She returned the smile but it soon vanished with the seriousness of the situation. The truth was he needed professional medical help but that wasn't always available when someone was hiking the trail.

"Is he dead?" Landon asked. Although he'd heard Billy stop breathing, he had to be sure. She nodded. "Good."

"Dakota, I need you to run to my backpack. There is a small first-aid kit in there. It's not much but it will do. I've got to clean and close this wound up."

"Close it?" Landon asked.

"Sew it shut."

"But has it hit an artery?" Dakota asked

"Arterial bleeding causes blood to spurt and it's bright red in color, there's no sign of that around or on him. Venous oozes out and is darker. That's what we're seeing. Usually you can stop it with pressure as long as there isn't a bleeding disorder or the person isn't on blood thinners. Landon?"

"No," he said.

She nodded and smiled. "Good."

Dakota took off running and Beth remained with Landon, applying pressure while Grizzly laid down and placed his head on Landon's leg. Beth looked at Grizzly. "Even he wants you to pull through." She stared at him. "Dakota said you crossed the river. For me."

"Yeah, I think I stubbed my toe on a rock," he said.

She burst out laughing as did he before groaning again.

Landon didn't manage to stay awake long enough to see Dakota return or feel the DIY repair that Beth performed on him a few miles from Caratunk, as shock set in and he eventually lost consciousness.

* * *

A warm band of summer light kissed his skin as the world snapped back into view. Landon's eyelids fluttered as he came to the awareness that he was in a hospital room. There was no beeping. Nothing monitoring him, but he was tucked beneath blankets and Dakota was asleep in a comfortable chair beside him. His throat was dry and he had no recollection of how he got there or where he was. The room was simple. A single bed with gray blankets and white sheets. A three-drawer dresser across the room. A flat-screen TV on the wall, two side tables, one chair for a guest, a bathroom, and flowery drapes covered the window. Attempting to shift into a raised position, he felt a twinge of lower pain. Instinctively he reached out and that's when he noticed a tube was in his arm. "Dakota."

She looked up and smiled. "Hey. How do you feel?"

"Better, I guess."

"You've been asleep for almost two days. I thought you'd never wake up."

His brow furrowed. "Where am I?"

"Northern Light Dean Hospital in Maine. It's about thirty miles east of Caratunk."

"Thirty miles?"

"Yeah, there was a guy in town with an old truck that

still worked. He was kind enough to give us a ride. If he hadn't, I think we would have lost you. After the bullshit we've been through, it kind of restored my hope in humanity again."

"A truck?"

She screwed her face up. "You don't remember?"

He shook his head.

"Strange, as you were talking some of the time. Your eyes opened. I mean I couldn't make sense of what you were saying but still... Huh! Crazy. You don't remember crossing the river?"

His memory was a blur. "No."

"Maybe best. Let me tell you it wasn't easy. Carrying you between me and Beth. You should seriously consider losing some weight." She chuckled.

"Where's Beth?"

Dakota lowered her chin.

"Dakota. Where's Beth?" he said in a firm tone.

"She went on. To Mount Katahdin."

"You're joking, right?"

"No. The doctor. I mean, the nurse who is assisting said you would probably need to rest for a week. The summit is roughly seventy miles from here. Beth figured she could make it there in three and a half days and be back before you got out. Don't worry, she took Grizzly with her."

He glanced to his side and saw an IV pole.

"They had to give you some blood. The rest is just fluids. Gravity does the work."

"But they didn't know what my blood type was?"

"You have Beth to thank for that. Your wallet."

"But I lost that a long time ago."

"Girl has a good memory. She remembered your blood type on the donor card in there. Do you want a drink?"

He nodded.

"I'll be right back."

She walked out of the room and returned a few minutes later with a female dressed in scrubs. "Ah, Mr. Gray. I'm glad to see you awake. How do you feel?"

"Good."

"It will still take some time but you should be set to leave at the end of the week."

"How are you still operating?"

"Poorly," the doctor replied. "We don't have power at all so we do the best we can with what we have. You were lucky you got here as fast as you did. You lost quite a bit of blood. However, your daughter did a great job of sewing you up. I think if she hadn't done that…"

"She's not my daughter."

"Oh?" The doctor looked at Dakota for confirmation. She shook her head.

"Well, your friends saved your life."

The doctor went through some routine checks, like listening to his heart, taking his pulse and temperature, and shining a small light in his eyes and ears before telling him to rest. After she left, Dakota handed him a canister of water and he chugged it down fast then wiped his lips with the back of his hand.

"How did they keep the blood cool without power?" Landon asked.

"Solar powered blood bank refrigerators."

"Well thank God for that."

Dakota smiled. "They have magazines here if you want to read," she said, handing him a cooking magazine. He snorted and she chuckled. "It's either that or I rattle on and you listen to my life story but I'm sure you wouldn't want to hear that." She laughed as she thumbed through a home magazine.

"Actually I would."

She looked up at him with a raised eyebrow "Really?" she said in a surprised tone.

"Well, as long as it doesn't involve hiking, rivers, knives or crazed lunatics, sure. We've got time to kill, right?"

"That we do."

Epilogue

He thought the day would never come. Excitement overwhelmed Landon upon seeing the first road sign for Castine just on the outskirts of Orland.

As promised, and to his relief, Beth and Grizzly had returned a week later, unharmed, from Mount Katahdin. He could have reamed her out for making him worry but he was just grateful to see her alive and well.

They had plenty of time to listen to her harrowing tales of her trip up the summit as it took them almost five days of hiking from the hospital to reach Hancock County.

Now with over a thousand miles behind them, seven months since the blackout, and only a few miles from Castine, he tried not to get his hopes up on the final stretch. "Okay, so you have freaked us out enough with the crazy group you managed to elude in Baxter State Park but what about the mountain?" Dakota asked. "Was it everything you expected it to be?" Dakota walked side by side with her. Landon looked over his shoulder at the two of them.

"I guess," Beth replied.

"You guess?" Landon chimed in. "What's that supposed to mean?"

She shrugged. "I don't know. I don't know what I was expecting. The view was beautiful."

Landon laughed. "That's it? The view was beautiful." He burst out laughing. "Well of course it was but what about that moment? You made it. You did what you set out to do, Beth. I would have thought you would have more to say."

"I figured I would too. You know, I built it up as this big thing in my mind, that once I reached the end I would somehow feel..."

"Whole?" Landon asked.

She nodded. "Yeah. Something like that." She exhaled hard. "I mean, don't get me wrong — it was everything and more. Exhausting, liberating and meaningful. It was truly incredible to reach the end and feel the wind whipping at my clothes as I stood beside the sign and looked out over Maine... but... the strangest thing is..."

"What?" he probed.

"Well, it wasn't my father who came to mind as much as it was... you. I wanted you there."

"Me?" Landon asked, raising an eyebrow.

"Yeah. Weird, huh?"

Dakota chuckled. "I dunno, it doesn't sound weird to me." She smiled at them both.

Landon felt honored but slightly awkward, so he quickly shifted the attention away from him. "And what about you, Grizzly? Did you enjoy it?" he asked as if the dog could understand.

Grizzly barked and wagged his tail.

Landon looked back at Beth. "Well, maybe at some point we'll both go up. How about that?"

"You'd do that?"

"Unwillingly, yeah, but I'd do it," he said with a chuckle. "After what we've been through I think I could handle anything."

They pressed on down Route 166 which was set back from the coastline, and he took in the familiar sights and smell of Penobscot Bay. "I used to take my kids out there," he said pointing to Fort Point Lighthouse across the bay. "Has some great spots for fishing. I think you guys are gonna love this place."

Their optimism soon faded as they reached the intersection of Wadsworth Cove Road and 166. There was a checkpoint up ahead, a Humvee with multiple armed men. The entire section of road was blocked off with an eighteen-wheeler, concrete barriers and rolled barbed wire. Had they not seen similar situations on the outskirts of towns across America, they might have thought it was strange.

"That's far enough!" one of the soldiers bellowed raising a hand and stepping forward. "What's your business?"

"I'm from Castine. My family lives here."

"Yeah. Who?"

"Sara Gray."

The soldier went over to a Humvee where a door was open. A guy in the driver's seat had his eyes closed and looked to be sleeping. The soldier gave him a shake and his eyes opened. He whispered in his ear and then turned and asked for a name.

"Landon Gray," he replied.

"And the other two?"

"Friends of mine."

The soldier nodded and got on a two-way radio. There was a lot of back and forth before they were told to take a seat at the edge of the road and wait. "You ever seen these guys before?" Beth asked.

"No. Then again, I didn't exactly get involved in the community."

About twenty minutes passed before three horses came galloping up to the checkpoint. Landon squinted but the glare from the sun made it hard to see who was on horseback. The soldier pointed to them and the horses came around the concrete barrier.

"Landon?"

He squinted, recognizing the voice but unable to see his face as the sun was shining in his face. "Carl?"

Carl hopped off his horse and greeted him with a handshake. "You've been gone a long time."

"Seven months," Landon replied.

"Has it been that long?"

"About that." His eyes drifted over the other riders. One of them looked familiar but he couldn't remember his name. The other was a stranger.

"This is Deputy Sam Daniels," Carl said, gesturing to the guy who looked familiar.

Sam gave a nod and adjusted himself on the horse. "How are you, Landon?"

"Good." He looked back at Carl. "Sara. Is she..?"

He was nervous to ask.

"Still alive. And your son too," Carl said. "They are something else. Strong people, I mean."

"Yeah. That's them."

Sam cast his gaze over the other two. "And who…?"

Landon twisted. "Oh sorry, this is Beth Sullivan and Dakota Larson. Friends of mine."

The dog barked.

"Let's not forget Grizzly," Beth said with a smile.

"Of course, sorry, my friend," Landon said bending to ruffle his hair.

Sam tipped his wide-brimmed hat. "Pleased to meet you."

Carl couldn't take his eyes off Landon. "Where have you been?"

"North Carolina."

"That's a long way. How did you get here?"

"Hiked. If you can believe that," Landon replied.

"You hiked all the way from North Carolina?"

He smiled and looked at Beth who shifted from one foot to the next. "On the AT."

Carl's eyebrows went up. "But that's wild country. You wouldn't even come hunting with me."

"I know, right. Crazy shit. And that's not the half of it. But I'll tell you more later. You think..." He motioned to the horses and Carl nodded.

"Yeah sure, come on up. We'll take you home."

Dakota and Beth got on the back of the other horses and they broke into a trot. Grizzly ran alongside.

"How are things?" Landon asked.

Carl sighed. "A lot has changed, Landon. A lot. And not all for the better, but I'm sure Sara will bring you up to speed."

They galloped down 166 which soon turned into Battle Avenue and Landon took in the sights of home. The once picturesque town now resembled a war zone. Buildings had been reduced to rubble, some homes were no more than charred remains and locals they saw along the way looked on with nervous eyes. Still, it felt good to put the trail behind them and be home, whatever that meant. "Oh, by the way, Sara took people in, so don't be surprised if you find your home a little crowded."

"That sounds like her. Business as usual."

"I guess," Carl replied casting a glance at Sam.

He had a sense that Carl was privy to things he wasn't.

He wasn't sure whether to be worried or not.

As the Manor Inn came into view, a sense of relief washed over him. It was really over. All that hiking, all that time in the backwoods, all those troubles were behind him. Finally he could rest. It was good to see his estate was still in one piece. A number of people were outside, a guy hanging up washing on a line, a couple bringing horses into the barn that he'd used for rebuilding a classic car. It was a 1956 Austin Healey. As they passed the open doors, he noticed it wasn't in there.

"You can drop us here," he said. "That's good."

Landon dismounted and brushed himself off. He really needed a bath.

"I'll swing by later. We'll have a drink. Catch up," Carl replied.

"Sounds good," he reached up and shook his hand. "Thanks again."

The deputies waved them off and he took a deep breath as he looked up at the house. "Home. I can barely believe we made it."

"How do you feel?" Beth asked.

"Nervous."

She slipped her arm around his. "Well, I'm right here with you."

He gave her hand a squeeze and they made their way around to the side door. The first person he saw when he entered was Rita Thomas. She had a little baby in her arms and was rocking the child back and forth. "Landon?"

"Hey Rita."

She looked shocked and opened her mouth to say something but nothing came out.

"Sara. She around?"

As if on autopilot, Rita lifted a finger pointing to the sunroom without looking that way. "Come on. I can't wait for you to meet her," Landon said bringing Beth down the hallway through the kitchen where he saw a few strangers. He continued on toward a pair of double glass doors that led into the sunroom. His face was beaming as he opened the door and stepped in. It soon faded as he looked upon Sara kissing Jake Parish.

"Sara?"

As she turned out of his arms, her eyes widened and all the blood drained from her face. Sara took a few steps in his direction and looked as if she'd seen a ghost. "Landon?"

His eyes bounced between them and hers between him and Beth.

* * *

THANK YOU FOR READING

All That Escapes Book 3

All That Rises Book 4 Available Oct 2019

Please take a second now to leave a review. Even a few words is really appreciated. Thanks kindly, Jack.

About the Author

Jack Hunt is the author of horror, sci-fi and post-apocalyptic novels. He currently has over thirty books published. Jack lives on the East coast of North America. If you haven't joined Jack Hunt's Private Facebook Group you can request to join by going here. https://www.facebook.com/groups/1620726054688731/ This gives readers a way to chat with Jack, see cover reveals, and stay updated on upcoming releases. There is also his main Facebook page if you want to browse that.

www.jackhuntbooks.com

jhuntauthor@gmail.com

Made in the USA
Coppell, TX
04 February 2020